Mass Appeal

The Ghost

 Against All Oddz Publications

Against All Oddz Publications
North Chesterfield, Virginia

Published by Against All Oddz Publications.

Web: www.theghoststories.webs.com

ISBN 978-1466424951

Interior design and layout by: Glenda Wallace at interiorbookdesigns.com

Cover designed by: Keith Saunders at mariondesigns.com

For distribution information and bulk ordering:

Against All Oddz Publications

P.O. Box 37085

North Chesterfield VA 23234

ISBN 978-1466424951

Thirteenth Amendment to the United States Constitution

Neither slavery nor involuntary servitude, except as a punishment for crime whereof the party shall have been duly convicted, shall exist within the United States, or any place subject to their jurisdiction.

The Fame is not my aim

Greater there is in you

If you only knew ...

The Ghost

Prologue

"For God sakes man, do you even realize what you've done? All the people who's suffering as a result of this senseless war you've started."

"Senseless."

"Damn it man, you must listen to me!" Kihiem urged as the intensity in his voice sparked with each word he spoke.

I understood Brother Minister's concern and his urgency in trying to bring about peace to this chaotic situation that we found ourselves in. So I remained on the line well aware that our discussion was being monitored by the relentless CIA and possibly every other damn Government Agency in the country. At this point, it really didn't matter much, because this thread mill ride that I was on was just about to be over. In fact, I could feel the cowards moving in on me..

Kihiem continued, "Nat, look my brother...Lets reason together. There is only one way this story is gonna end. Do you hear me man, one way! And that is with you dead in a fuckin' body bag just like the others. Why don't you just come in man? It's not too late for you; it doesn't have to end this wa-

"But it must end this way, brother," I reply.

"They're going to shoot you down like a dog in the streets!"

"I won't be the first nor will I be the last. Don't you understand...Kihiem; you of all people should know that the price of freedom is death."

"And what about the others Nat, did you even give them a choice?"

"You know your history brother. People die in war. Somebody must die in order for truth to be established."

"Truth brother...is that what you think you are bringing about? Tell me what truth have you established Nat? You call this truth, sacrificing the lives of innocent people... You know what they say about the blind man Nat, don't you."

"That those who follow him will fall in a ditch along with that blind man," I finished Brother Minister's statement. *"Is that how you see me Brother Kihiem...as a blind man?"*

"I just don't understand your thinking. What do you expect to accomplish?"

"Well it's quite simple brother... The only thing that America understands is violence. So I am only here to serve as a warning... that until my people receive their just due, which is complete freedom, justice and equality then in every generation there will be a Nat Turner rising up and raising HELL!"

Introduction to Mass Appeal

V ery early in life, I can recall cruising through Baltimore's degenerating slums in one of my smoked filled, fly European cars while Minister FM's powerful and captivating voice penetrated my ear drums. While most of my peers would be riding to the latest sounds from whatever hot rapper who was out at that time, I'd find myself some of that good green stuff, pop in a cassette tape by Minister FM and ride man. Some may question my getting coma toasted while listening to the Minister. It's crazy right, but what the hell can I say. I was a lost soul living in darkness, searching for light. I had never heard anyone preach as he did, with so much fire and vigor. And though I was knee deep in the streets, committing every sin under the sun, little did I know that a seed was being planted inside me. I must admit that prior to me being exposed to lectures by the Minister, I like many others had my own perception about the Islam Nation. I thought they were cons who robbed their own people. I thought they were gangsters in bowties who assassinated Brother Malcolm back in the day. There are so many others who may feel the same. But that is what happens when we allow outsiders to think for us and write our history.

I know what some of you are probably thinking, but rest assure, I'm not a preacher about to teach a sermon. Far from a saint, what I am about to give you is Real talk…A story that has yet to be told by one who has lived the life that a lot of our young rappers glorify in their songs. But there's no glory for a hustler. Eventually my illegal activities would soon catch up with me. The FBI intercepted three kilos from my lieutenant

coming through Miami International Airport, they applied
some pressure on him and the rest is history. From that
moment on, my fate was sealed. In just a matter of months,
they brought my entire drug operation to a screeching halt.
The end result was a first class trip to Federal Prison where I
was to serve nearly a life sentence. Though I lived the life of a
boss on the street, I learned instantaneously from the horrific
experience (prison life) that I was just a mere worker. I went
from having it all, to having nothing. But later for that, I feel
no need to bore you with another lame story about the rise
and fall of a "Husterling Legend". Instead, let's chop it up
about something real for a minute. By the way, I go by the
name of Nathaniel Turner, but all of my friends call me Nat.
Originally from Baltimore Maryland; my parents migrated
down to Hampton Virginia when I was just a young boy.

Virginia was very interesting, particularly my first day in
junior high school. Mrs. Stevens, my fifth period history
teacher gave me the most startling expression after I was
asked to stand before the class and state my full name. When
class was finally over, Mrs. Stevens asked me to stay back, I
did. She was an itty bitty woman in her late 50's, or possibly
early 60's with silverish, shoulder length hair, wrapped in a
long ponytail. As I grabbed a seat in front of her desk, I
watched her as those unreadable beady little eyes stared back
at me through a set of wire framed glasses. She suddenly
begins to acquire about my background, where I was from and
who my parents were and so on. Then out of the blue she asks,
"You're not by any chance a descendent of Nat Turner are
you?" She smiled awkwardly at me as I sat there looking
clueless as to the nature of our discussion. At that time, the
only person I knew of that went by such a name was I. During

our brief talk, it became obvious to me that there was more that meets the eye behind this mysterious character that coincidently possessed the exact same name as I. So out of curiosity, I asked her about this guy. I will never forget how distorted her face became; how her wrinkled pale skin flushed hot pink. Her response was short and blunt. In her words, there was nothing about Nat Turner that I needed to know; all except that he was a monster who did some very horrible things. And that was about it before she kicked me out and instructed me to go to sixth period. But her response didn't set well with me. In fact, it only incited my desire to know more which at that young age seemed like I was fighting an uphill battle because no one ever took me serious. At just the mention of his name, folks would simply tense up. My teachers were always curious of why I was so interested and in many instances; they'd make me feel as though I was committing some heinous crime for inquiring about this guy. I mean, they made Nat Turner out to be a real life boogie man of some sort. In those days information on him was scarce, which in my humble opinion was done on purpose. After a while, I eventually lost interest and started to focus my attention on other less productive things. It wouldn't be until a few years later that I'd finally have the information to do an in depth study on my distant brother, Nat Turner. But by that time, I'd be far removed from free society and left with nothing but time…and lots of it.

Resurrection...
A Young Man's Journey From
Confinement, To Enlightment

I t took a while for me to get adjusted to my new reality (prison life). Like a dope-addict having to detoxify from the monstrous grip of heroin, I on the other hand had to tangle with the (ill street blues). You know, being deprived of everything that had once sustained me. The cash, the women, the life! It was all now a thing of the past. The prison was crammed with youngsters like me. We did anything to past time, whether it was gambling, or smoking on some good bud just to chase off the pains. I watched lots of television and indulged myself in day to day sport and play which was to the institutions delight. And please don't buy into the hype of prison being a place of rehabilitation. The true criminals who ran the prison industry and had capital invested in our bound bodies being confined, could give a rat's ass if we rehabilitated and strived to become productive members of our community. There aren't any real educational programs, or job training to assist a brother whose trying to reenter society on a positive note. So those of us who don't take out the time to improve and take the initiative to educate ourselves to higher levels of consciousness, will slowly just wither away like that once beautiful flower that languishes from the lack of sunlight. Sadly, that just so happened to be me for the first five years of my sentence...however, there was a turning point for me.

As long as I have breath in my body, I will never ever forget this day. It was approximately, 5:30pm, March 5, 2000, Tuesday evening. I made a call to my parents and as expected my old man answered the telephone. The moment I heard his voice, I regretted that I'd even called. You see, my mom, God bless her soul had been undergoing Chemo treatment for the past month and the doctors were indicating that her condition wasn't improving. In fact, it was getting worse with time because the cancer had spread throughout 60% of her body. So because of the bad news, I hadn't talked to my family for almost three weeks because it was just too damn depressing for me. But on that day, I called. Pops is a man of the steel, the strength of our family but on this particular day, he cried like I had never heard a person cry before in my life. My mom was on her death bed, slipping in and out of consciousness. Only 45 years old, she was so young. My dad said that her doctor informed him that it was a good possibility that she wouldn't make it through the week. I hung up the telephone. By the time I called back, which was the very next day, it was already too late because mama had passed some time during the night. Mama and I were like two bonded siblings, she was my best friend in the whole world, so you can imagine how pained I was over losing her.

That same day but later in the evening, I can remember sitting out on the softball field alone. Lots of brothers were out that day but in the morbid mind state that I was in, I didn't see any of them. I was in my own little miserable world, plus I had smoke some bud so I was floating on cloud nine. For hours, I sat and wept while thinking and reminiscing about mama. I didn't even realize how high I'd gotten until I attempted to stand and couldn't. Recall was announced over the intercom for all inmates to clear the yard and return to their perspective Housing Unit. The way my head spun in circles and not to mention my eyes being bloodshot red, there was no way I'd make it across the compound without catching a ticket (officer pulling me over). I was already on the SIS hot list for marijuana sales in the prison so most of the officers knew me. I carefully maneuvered my way up to the front gate, merging in with a sea of other brothers in a attempt to stay out of the eyesight of the redneck officer posted up to my right. But no matter how much I seemed to hide myself, I could sense him on to me. I could actually feel his hawking eyes burning a hole straight through me. Heartbeat drumming and paranoid as ever, I proceeded with the pack of noisy inmates, when suddenly a figure fell in beside me, gave me a friendly pat on the back then told me to be cool. I recognized him instantly from his clean shave and kind demeanor that he was no doubt an Islam Nation soldier. The book in his hand, he quickly pushed it in my direction, insisted that I take it and pretend as if I were reading. The Islam Nation had a lot of clout on the compound and many officers showed the brothers of peace, respect. I know this for a fact to be true, especially after making it pass that bull headed cop and not being hassled. Once we were clear, the brother whose name happened to be Rodney X told me to hold on to his book and suggested that I read it. 'Fair enough,' I thought. It was the least I could do for him bailing me out like he did. Then before we parted ways, he looked into my swollen red eyes and said, "Brother, Allah doesn't put on us a burden that is too much to bear." He said those words to me and turned on his heels real smooth like. For the first time since I'd been holding it, I flipped the book over and glanced at its cover. It was the Message to the Black Man.

I had always admired the Muslims for their outstanding contributions and consistency in trying to bring forth awareness to our hopeless communities. As far back as I could remember, I know of no other organizations that have been more effective in helping cultivate and bring out the best in black folk's other than the Islam Nation. I can recall some of my closest homeboys as we were coming up, converting over to Islam. Whatever the hell it was in that message, it changed them instantly. Whatever it was, I wanted to no parts of it. I was too caught up in the street life. And though I had an immense deal of respect for them, I can't say that I agreed with their economical tactics. There I was out there, stunting in my top notch foreign vehicles, draped in the finest tailored made linens and hanging out with some of the prettiest dime sexes that any playa would want to feast their eyes on. Then I'd run into my used to be homey's who'd decided to trade in a lavish lifestyle to post up in 90% weather in a hot ass suit and bowtie. But they were content, I couldn't get it. Hell, I was six figures and running and well on my way to becoming a young millionaire and yet, I was a long ways from being content. So many things I didn't understand in my ignorance. Unbeknownst to my comrades, I got my hands on some of Minister FM's lectures. From the moment I heard his voice and listened to the things he had to say, I couldn't stop thinking about him. But then just two months later the feds indicted me. I ended up in federal prison and five years into my sentence, I met back up with the Islam Nation. After reading 'Message to the Black Man' and really absorbing in the contents of that book, that same incredible grip-hold that took over me when listening to the Minister years prior, had revisited me again. However, even with the Minister in one ear trying to show me the light, I was fighting a losing battle inside my head. Engulfed by depression and extreme bitterness from losing my mom, not to mention being denied to even pay my last respect at her funeral service, I began to harbor sickening, violent thoughts. I was a walking time bomb amongst my prison peers, an accident just waiting to happen. I wanted to inflict bodily harm on somebody, or anybody for that matter. But the funny thing about it was, as much as I despised the prison heads for their insensitivity, my anger wasn't necessarily directed at them. It was the brothers around me, who I wanted to hurt, maim and at times even kill. I had not the slightest idea where this rage and misplaced hatred had stemmed from. Yet, it was there and the damn monster wouldn't go away. I know now that Allah (God) or whatever names that you may want to refer to Him as, was indeed watching over me and protecting me from my own destructive self. Whenever I would attempt to even act out my foolish thoughts, out of nowhere, an angel would appear.

One beautiful Saturday morning, I arose earlier than usual and decided to take a morning stroll. Upon reaching the rac yard and observing how lovely a day it was, I grabbed a seat on the first available bench that I saw. The sun shinned with such magnificence and the sky was clear and as blue as the Atlantic. To the right of me, was a guy whom all of the brothers referred to as Bird Man, particularly because of his unusual connection with birds. This guy could actually communicate with them and on any given day, it was nothing to find a flock of birds following him across the compound. It's somewhat amazing what a man would come to appreciate when he's confined and locked away long enough. It wasn't long before I found myself sneaking bread out of the dining hall to feed the birds which prior to my conviction was unheard of. I had no respect whatsoever for the small creatures of nature; however, time has a way of changing a man. While in the same process of me developing this new found adoration for these extraordinary creatures, I also envied the immeasurable freedoms that they possessed to soar the heavens and view the world from a whole other perspective. I would sat there on that bench in awe and admire God's wonderful creation while in the very same instant, wishing like hell that it was I who could spread out my wings and vacate this concrete jungle. And then there were those other moments where the sorrow and bitterness of my present situation would overwhelmingly invoke me to anger. The rage inside my chest would build and swell to capacity as all sound around me would cease. My eyes would transform into little beads of fire and the guys in my midst would become faceless. My attitude would suddenly lock into destroy mode. I can't adequately explore how this monster would embody me and in the blink of an eye, suborn my pure thoughts into something envenomed by hatred. A disease in my heart maybe, I don't know.

It was on a day like the one just described, sitting alone on my favorite bench, spaced out in a trance when unexpectedly a familiar voice says almost in a subtle whisper "Rise above your emotions brother and into the thinking of God." Instantly, the gloom and discontentment that just only a moment ago, had pinned me down immediately dispersed. At the mere presence of this beautiful brother, a wide grin took the place of my frown and I couldn't help but laugh, because this was not the first time Rodney X found me trapped inside a maze of confusion. In spite of how some may perceive the brothers in the Islam Nation as being extremist and unapproachable, Rodney X; however had a way of making everyone around him comfortable. He was very down to earth and wise beyond years. I thought he was my own personal angel, because he'd always seem to show up at the right time. That day on the rac yard, he joined me on the bench and we sat and conversed until it was time to leave. A lot was said between us, but what stuck out the most to me was his insight on "Anger". He explained to me that anger was a degenerating emotion that crippled one's ability to think rationally. He added that an idle mind was the devils workshop, then he went on to suggest that I get away from self pity and try to focus on doing something more productive with my time. And it all made perfect sense. I mean like, what the hell was I doing anyway. Around me, it seemed as though everything was in constant motion, except for me. My mom was long gone and she wasn't coming back. My greatest obstacle was allowing certain conditions beyond my control to overwhelm me with worry. I finally had to come to grips with the realization that in order for me to even begin to consider a future for myself, I had to first let go of the past. It was no good to me anymore. Rodney X help me to see that the only thing in this world that I truly had power to change, was me. And boy, I was a piece of work. But I was dissatisfied with the man in the mirror and it's said that dissatisfaction is supposed to bring about change, something new and most certainly better. Already, I'd lost five years of precious time, which could have been used more constructively.

That following Friday, I was invited out to my very first study group session held inside the prisons Chapel Department. Although it was a very different experience for me, I was impressed. The brothers and their polite mannerisms and how each of them received me with open arms, just made me feel as though I was amongst family. Originally, the class was designed to build human potential and spark conversation amongst the brothers. As expected when a new comer enters the circle, everyone is instructed to state their first name. When it was my turn to introduce myself to the group, I got that same reaction that I always got whenever I would say my name. But on the contrary, from the misinformation that I'd been getting throughout my life, these brothers expressed different views about the so called Boogie Man, (Nat Turner). For starters, he wasn't the horrible monster that my childhood teacher once described him as. Reflecting back, it was not a good time for black folks in those days. Racist white, bigots had their way with us. They broke up families, raped our mothers and slaughtered strong black men before their families like one would do cattle. Slavery was so ugly that many of us nowadays would rather pretend that it didn't exist. And it was this ugly injustice being carried out against black people all over the country that caused Nat Turner's blood to boil. So as a result of the brutal white domination, Nat assembled together a hit squad, all with the common goal to annihilate their enslavers. The journey was a murderous one. Everything white and not right, these brothers cut down including children and babies.

My faithful readers, I can almost guess what some of you are probably thinking right about now. He's a monster! Why would he do such a thing? What did the children do?? Well,

Nat Turner's mind set was that he felt that the only way that White Supremacy was to remain dominate over his people, was if that same demonic mindset be taught to the enslavers children. So Nat and his small army decided that the world could do without another tainted minded child who would only grow up to oppress him and his people. I'm in no position to judge whether Nat Turners method of action was right or wrong; however as cruel as his actions may seem, it is an unfortunate part of our history. A history that I felt needed to be established before I dive deeper into my story. For those who may not be familiar with the historical Nat Turner, I just wanted to give you a little bit of him because if one doesn't know what was, meaning (history), then one won't know what is meaning (future). And what is…is me. The second coming…..The future.

Trust me; it's not at all what you think. This story is not about black men invading the suburbs and slaughtering little white children, so rid yourselves of such foolish thinking. This tale is about the rise and fall of one of the most powerful black organizations to ever be established in North America. But wait…its only right that I start from the beginning, so that you can be a witness to my transformation, which actually began at my first study group session. In fact, I was so enthused about learning something new, that the following week at service, I stood up and became a believer. If I was going to try and make a change for the better then there was no need to waist anymore time. I didn't care what anyone had to say, or how foolish I may have looked in the eyes of others for accepting the truth. I know that the Islam Nation's message had healing powers because within the next few weeks of me joining, I could feel a change taking place inside me. And it showed outwardly because all of a sudden, I didn't want to participate in old self destructive habits. You know, inhaling in the poisons, killing precious brain cells by getting toasted off of marijuana smoke. I began to see myself in an entirely different light. My next order of business was cleaning up my foul mouth. I was one who could hardly speak without the use of profanity. I was also one who gave women hell. When discussing the opposite sex, it seemed like every other word that would leave my mouth would be Bitch or Hoe. I was pretty damn pathetic. Didn't really know any better. In my studies, I learned that black women imparticular, but all women in general are worth so much more than what we try and reduce them to. She's a life giver, the very first teacher of the child and the strength that has been holding us brothers down ever since our sojourn into this stranger's land. There's nothing new under the sun.

So now that the Government bad boxed me in, restrained my movements, it was the perfect opportunity for me to make the most out of the time that I had on my hands. Malcolm X was one of my greatest inspirations. Like me, he was a street cat and one whom society had deemed an outcast, yet with all the barricades of bullshit in his path, he overcame all odds. I did an intense study on this brother. The Webster dictionary soon became my closest ally. I read the book from cover to cover, and every other piece of literature that I could get my hands on to help broaden my vocabulary. Inside the prison, brothers who'd known me prior to my coming into the life saving teachings of the Islam Nation, all gave me props and congratulated me on my remarkable transformation from a state of mental death into one of life. But of course, there were those who condemned and ridiculed my sincere efforts. My so called comrades who I would once run the yard with, blowing chronic smoke and shooting the breeze about bitches and hoes, wasn't feeling my move.

They liked me better when I was down in hell with them. A wise brother said to me once that anything or anyone who doesn't encourage the good in you and tries to hinder productivity should automatically be cut off. Whatever that thing was, it would do more harm than good. I took that advice to heart. I began to study hard and dive deeper into the Islam Nation's teachings as well as other aspects of literature that pertained to history. I was all for the principles instilled in us by Minister FM to do for self and not expect someone else to do for us what we should be doing for ourselves. I loved that concept! Hell, one of the reasons I sold drugs in the first place was because I didn't want to do slave labor to make another man wealthy. But in prison, I found out first hand just what true slave labor was. There I was an inmate, which in all truth was just another name for slave. If only the elders could see us now, their grand babies being subjected to the very same wicked system that grossly enslaved them in a relentless attempt to crush their courageous African spirits. Surely their precious souls are not at rest. From the grave, I often hear the wrangling cries of freedom. My mind constantly ranges back and forth through uncounted generations and I feel all that they ever felt, but double. So many painful years of being trampled upon and still we rise.

I quickly moved up through the ranks and in no time, I was referred to by my prison peers as the fiery young Minister of the Islam Nation. Me being a walking example of how God could raise the dead to life, make the blind see and the deaf hear, I was able to draw many young brothers to the Mosque.

Some of whom were the very same cats that clowned me before my resurrection. The gangbangers and what not... they were brothers who prior to their imprisonment, terrorized their own neighborhoods and degraded their women. Brothers who'd fathered illegitimate children only to abandon them, they all came out to the Mosque in droves, hoping to hear a word that would speak to their troubled hearts. I understood them and knew exactly what they needed. They were men, warriors who if given a chance and the proper guidance, could blossom into productive soldiers and possibly potential leaders of their communities. I was honored beyond words and deeply humbled to stand before them as a shining example of how God could change a man's heart.

If only my mom was alive, she'd be so proud. As for my pops, it took him years to accept my new faith being a bonafide Christian and all. Like a lot of black folks, he viewed the Islam Nation through the lens of a corrupt media. Why so much dislike towards an organization that had done nothing but good for our people and the country as a whole. Why do we hate the unknown and fear what we don't understand. In other words, my old man didn't know squat about that which he claimed to dislike. (The Islam Nation) But eventually, I won him over. I had to explain to him that, Muslims and Christians are just mere titles that keep us divided into different sects. All that should matter pops is that I am a better man today because of the decision I made to join the Islam Nation. Over the next few years, I would continue to excel in knowledge as I went about my never ending mission to spread inspiration to the brothers. But around my tenth year in confinement, I became aware of something happening inside the prison that was very unsettling for me. With each year that passed, the faces pouring through the prison gates looked younger and younger.

Newcomers would come in fresh from off the streets, green as the grass and fall victim to the many pitfalls of prison life. If it wasn't the gambling, or dabbling in drugs then homosexuality was like a growing epidemic inside the walls. The prisons had become a breeding ground for such behavior. And let's not forget about the vast gang initiations where they recruited guys faster than you could blink. So with those challenges before us, it was definitely a struggle for us in the Islam Nation to reach our young brothers with a positive message. I wouldn't go so far as to say that we were fighting a losing battle, but it sure was an uphill one. For the most part, the Brotherhood had many supporters amongst our fellow prisoners. Even those who were not in agreement with our beliefs still respected us nonetheless. From my close observation, I learned while a lot of brothers believed in the truth that we represented, what kept many of them from not joining on was our restrictive laws and strict discipline, in which we as believers were bound under! The rules were our success. In a world where wrong had been made fair seeming, the restrictive laws were like our body armor that protected us from the evil that surrounded us. Religion had failed the majority of these brothers and life had put a pretty good beaten on them. Though, the Brotherhood worked hard and diligently to enlightened and encourage our brothers to strive to improve themselves, for many of these guys, it was more like preaching to a choir. They weren't trying to hear nothing about rehabilitation and mind elevation. So years upon years and to the institutions delight, we'd engage in frivolous prison sport and play, entertain countless hours of BET and numerous other trivial affairs of which was of no real significance to self development. As a result of this wasted time and energy, the prison house had become a revolving door for many. It literally made me sick to my stomach as I was forced to watch helplessly as this pathetic scene would replay itself over and over. If only they would just listen to what we had to say. Adhere to the wicked, Governmental created circumstances in which caused us to result to desperate measures to support our families by any means.

It finally became apparent to me that the Islam Nation alone couldn't do this. We were losing too many sol-diers....Strange things began happening to me during this time. One imparticular was this recurring dream of me on some remote plane watching the sun rise and set. Every single freaking day for nearly a whole week, these bizarre images would disrupt my sleep. In the beginning, I tried to brush it off as some crazy coincidence, but in the back of my mind, a very sound voice told me to look more deeply in to it. Well, I tried that only to come up with absolutely nothing. But then one morning while I was dreaming this very same dream but instead of remaining asleep, I forced myself awake. The strangest thing occurred. It was like I had awakened to find myself in another dream. I could feel the prevailing heat of the sun as its strong rays penetrated the tiny opening, which was suppose to serve as my window. I was immediately drawn to the window where I stood, gaping at this giant ball of fire, shinning down on me with so great a magnificence that it appeared to be heavenly sent. I was frozen, staring at this thing until I was almost blinded. I was back in bed shortly after, but sleep only seemed to have eluded me, my mind was working.

The more I began to analyze and reflect over these recurring dreams, the more I felt as though there was some type of hidden message in them. You know, sort of like a Chinese fortune cookie. Then coincidently while I was sitting alone in my cell later in the afternoon, reading over my Study material in a desperate attempt to make sense of the strange and unknown, my cellmate Eddie of five years entered the room. When you're shacked up with someone for as long as Eddie and I had been, you become accustom to certain habits. I could always tell when something was bothering Eddie, his facial expression being a dead giveaway. I would soon learn that Eddie's youngest boy, who was just days away from his sixteenth birthday, had been brutally gunned down in the streets. But what was even more inconceivable, was the sad fact that the deadly bullet was not intended for the straight A student. Talk about tragedy, talk about a waste of potential. Imagine having to watch a grown man cry. Eddie blamed himself for his boy's untimely demise, saying that his presence there at home would have made all the difference...TRUE INDEED.

Our youth were dying in record numbers and it seemed like there was no end in sight. And though I was doing my best to reach out to brothers around me, still it just wasn't enough. This depressed the hell out of me. I had to figure out a way to get to these guys. The younger ones imparticular who normally wouldn't attend a Islam Nation service. While I sat there with Eddie, helping him to relieve his fatherly grief, I too felt the pain from the lost of this innocent kid. Struggling for a solution for what seemed to be an ever growing problem in our community, suddenly the idea of launching my own

organization for AT RISK Youth, popped in my mind. I wasn't
trying to create another I.N. although many of the principles I
learned would certainly be implemented in my program. Why
try to fix something that wasn't broken? I knew that my ideas
to build this dream of mine would possibly meet with some
opposition, particularly by members of the Brotherhood, so I
didn't break the news to anyone until I was absolutely confident of the direction in which I wanted to go.

A little later in the evening, I found myself in my usual
sanctuary, alone on the bench where I normally sat. The sun
was setting beatifically. And as I admired its majesty while in
the very same instant, contemplating over the death of Eddie's
son, tears suddenly commenced to stream down my cheeks. I
couldn't dismiss the disturbing images of this kid being cut
down so maliciously so soon. Pain burning my eyes, I stared at
the illuminating sun as it made its final descent. Then it hit
me…the meaning behind the mysterious dreams. The original
man was likening to the sun, dipped in black. But as the sun
was going down right before my eyes, so was an exceedingly
great number of our young black boys, caught up in a vicious
cross fire of self hatred which automatically resulted in gross,
self annihilation. I truly believe whole heartedly that the
recurring dreams along with Eddie's tragedy, among a few
other bizarre happenings, were all signs for me to pursue this
vision. That next morning, I awakened uttering the words,
"RISING SUN", which later would become the name of my
organization. The Islam Nation was already doing a superb
job in raising the awareness of our people, however; I just felt
that I could be more of service if I pursued a different course.
Unlike many of the other organizations, mines would target
just boys, particularly because it was the young black male

under vehement attack. By no means am I saying that our women weren't to a certain degree, but it was us being cut off from the job circuit. It was us being lynched in court rooms all across this rotten country. And it was us who corrupt cops sought to brutalize and shoot out right in the streets like dogs. But even a dog got a better day than us. As with my organization, the mission was still the same, nothing had changed, except the name. I had to use another method to reach my brothers who was slipping through the cracks, which meant that I had to lose the shiny shoes, strap my construction boots on and go down into the mud and get them. But of course, as I had anticipated, there were some members of the Brotherhood who were opposed to my making "RISING SUN" a reality.

I was accused of abandoning my post and reneging on my word to uphold the mission of Islam Nation. I tried with all sincerity to explain my intent, that this was no vain attempt but my actions were solely a reflection of my love for the mission. As intelligent as my brothers were, they just couldn't see the bigger picture. My heart was not deceiving me. These dreams weren't ordinary dreams void of substance, but they were divine visions filled with instructions. I was very sane, though there were some who would disagree. But I was certain that I was on to something because the force driving me was so great, that I felt it in the very essence of my soul. There would be no compromise with RISING SUN and if I made a judgment error in some way then let Allah be the judge. I expressed these thoughts with the Brotherhood in our last meeting as I was making my transition. My good friend and mentor, Rodney X approached me with his hand extended after the meeting had adjourned. As we shook hands and greeted, I could sense the disappointment in his saddened eyes as they seemed to penetrate the windows of my soul. There was no mistaken the love and companionship he had for his little brother. Someone who he'd molded from mere clay and help cultivate into something of value, similar to how a mother would nurture her own child. This was one of the hardest decisions I've ever had to make but life was full of adversity. Rodney X said to me as we were filing out of the Chapel Department that he couldn't believe that it had come to this. "How could you leave the Brotherhood, this is your salvation my brother, your life line. How could one survive without their life line...So this is it, huh? You're really stepping down."

Understanding would soon come to my brother. God created every man to be different, and although we all shared a common longing to see our people free from injustice and oppression, there was no one method to obtain such a goal. It took skill and clever tactics to reach a people who had been so messed over. So, where would I be if it wasn't for the Islam Nation? In all truth, I'd probably be somewhere drugged out, smoking marijuana and sneaking around, engaging in homosexual activities. I'm just keeping it one-hundred. This was a system designed to punk a brother out. So to my inquiring brothers who may want to know am I still in the Islam Nation...No I am not...the Islam Nation is inside me...

Chapter

1

"Nat Turner One Year Later"

Anything of value is worth fighting for. Many questioned my motives for leaving the Brotherhood and starting my own organization. They automatically assumed that my departure was the result of an internal problem within the Islam Nation that had finally come to a head. Some even felt as though my actions were a slap in the face to the existing Islam Nation on the compound. The prison media hyped it up, the administration hopped on the band wagon and sadly, some of my closest brothers even fed into the nonsense. And though this was disappointing to me, yet I understood that God had put this idea in my mind, not theirs. So under the brewing hostility and bubbling tension, I pressed on spreading the word about RISING SUN to anyone who would listen. Eddie and myself had flyers printed up, stating on them the organizations program in which we flooded the entire prison complex with. From the start, I knew that this would be a difficult mission. But also, I kept in mind that the creator didn't make mistakes. If I couldn't handle it, someone who could would've gotten the assignment. My roommate, Eddie was the first to join on to RISING SUN. In spite of his Christian beliefs and my religious preference, we could relate on so many levels.

In the Islam Nation we were being taught to love self and one another and not to allow artificial barriers to keep us away from our brothers and sisters who shared a different belief. Names and titles were insignificant in RISING SUN. Eddie and I and all future members would be brothers for the same struggle. Eddie was just as excited as I was to get the organization rolling. The death of his son had left him hollow and unbelievably bitter, which was expected. But as we started to see progress with the organization, I began to notice life seeping back into him. His dedication even surprised me at times, then one day he said to me that RISING SUN was a blessing from on high. That without it, he thinks he would've fallen apart. His son was gone, but through this organization we could possibly save the next kid from death or incarceration. I was in agreement with my brother. If done properly, RISING SUN had the potential to impact the prison in a major way and eventually the world at large.

In the beginning stages, we begin holding dialogue with a number of various gang members, particularly their leaders, so as not to disrespect anyone. I'd break down the ideology behind RISING SUN. Of course, some brothers thought I was nuts, possibly back puffing la la again. Yeah I was high alright, only it was a natural high and I was serious as a heart attack. A lot of cats couldn't get away with what I was doing. I was down in the trenches amongst real life hustlers and killers and real thug lifers, the so called worse of the worst. But they knew me, and respected me because just six years prior to my joining the Islam Nation, I was leading the pack in foolishness. These brothers had love for me, particularly because when I had first come in, I was still heavily connected to the streets and had the ability to make stuff happen, if you know what I mean. With the right inside man, I had drugs pouring through the prison for a number of years up until my transformation. So through our inner actions, I had built up a pretty good rapport with the gangs. But that was all in the history books now. I was now going to these brothers in an attempt to get them to call a truce between each other and then hopefully to unite under my organization. I know to some it may seem like a ridiculous thought, like maybe I was overstepping my bounds just a tad, but I don't believe in impossibility. In fact, I was taught to dream big and dare to be different and do exceptional things, to not be like the average Joe who simply went along just to get along. So in spite of how preposterous my intentions appeared to some of the vision-lackers, I was very optimistic about these rejected and despised brothers coming together. So with that said, my Chief Aid and I came up with an interesting strategy to rally brothers together. Already, we had spent nearly three to four months promoting our program and conversing with various gang members. For the most part, many of these cats were feeling RISING SUN. Not enough to join on, but they respected my mind and even encouraged me. Around this time, the organization had grown to fifteen members, including Eddie and myself. The next step was figuring out a way to bring all the brothers together in a peaceful setting. Sam, one of the newcomers suggested that we cook a feast and invite brothers out to the rac yard where we all could sit and politic over unifying. It was a damn good idea because if there was one thing I was sure of, brothers loved to eat. And we had some of the best cooks right there in our organization.

We set a date and immediately put the word out on the compound about our special gathering, which was one month away. During the next few weeks leading up to the event, I had been spending lots of time with the Islam Nation, sharing my ideas and hoping that they would support me in this venture. But some of my brothers still didn't get it. They couldn't yet see that what I was doing would eventually be good for our Nation as a whole. It seemed like the more success I had, the more distant the Brotherhood and I became. I never wanted us to fall out ever this. Our spiritual father, Minister FM was teaching us to not be surface dwellers. In order to gain a true understanding, we had to crack the surface of a thing, if as though we were dissecting a frog in biology class. If in fact my brothers weren't "Surface Dwellers" then they'd see that I was still holding firmly to my post. They would see that I hadn't stop performing my duty as a civilized man. But just because a person had eyes didn't mean that they could see…

The whole compound seemed to have come out to support our special event, accompanied by about thirty to forty officers who anticipated drama. None of us expected such a turn out but the mere sight of the immense gathering brought joy to my heart. The administration was on pens and needles having never seen so many rival gangs in one place at the same time, no chaos. The only disappointment of the night was the strong presence of the Islam Nation missing from the scene. I felt naked and exposed like Adam in the Garden of Eden. They were supposed to be there, I needed their support. But I had to suppress my emotions to be affective and accomplish what I set out to do. I wasn't alone, Allah was sufficient.

I ran down a long list of reasons why we should be together, why we should call a truce, and stop shedding one another's blood. I told the brothers that our real strength was in our numbers. If we unite and demand better treatment in the prison we won't be denied because we would be a strong force to be reckoned with. The more I talked, the more confident I became. Then half way through my lecture, I caught sight of Rodney X and about twenty soldiers in tow, maneuvering their way through a sea of bodies looking like a small army. I thought to myself, "Yeah, now that is the Islam Nation I know." In my Final address, I spoke specifically to the Bloods and Crips. I told them that we all have a common enemy and it sure ain't the brother standing next to them. While we're divided into sects, warring with one another, the real enemy is conquering us all. If we don't unite now…there is no future for us. RISING SUN is the future…We can make history right now, brothers. All you gotta do is Rise Sun and Step forward.

If you ask me, I did a hell of a job. But it wasn't enough to evoke brothers with in the Blood and Crip community to step up and join on to RISING SUN. There were, however two or three guys who came forth, but neither of them were in gangs. It was a start though. We would just have to continue pressing on and keep the pedal to the medal in trying to win our brothers over. I had been warned by numerous people that what I was doing could be considered as inciting a riot. I could be thrown into solitary or possibly shipped to another Institution. Majority of these little messengers were the scary, no back bone type cats who'd never stepped up for anything in their lives. I didn't care about any of that. Everybody can't be scared. Somebody had to stand up and rock the boat and create some waves. Why not me and why not now? Could you imagine the Bloods and Crips laying down their weapons and embracing one another to form a Brotherhood under RISING SUN? Join on to an organization that is designed to build human potential as well as counteract the Government-Assassins vicious plot to do our brothers in under the guise of "ANTI GANG UNIT." If we gave the Government back their guns, then they wouldn't have any justification in their planned slaughter of us in years to come. I believed that if we were successful inside the prisons, then eventually the word would leak out and the spirit of RISING SUN would touch our brothers on the outside. As unlikely as this vision may have seemed, it was never the less a vision that I was dedicated to making a reality.

"When a call comes along and you know in your bones that it is just, yet you refuse to defend it, at that moment you begin to die." I can't recall where I first read those profound words, but for me and the work that I was attempting to do, they struck a nerve. RISING SUN was the last thought in my mind before falling asleep at night and the first thought on my brain when I awaken. **IT WAS EITHER DO WHAT I WAS DOING OR DIE TRYING.** Those very words would almost prove to be prophetic in days to come. It was two days later to be exact. I woke up early as I did every other morning, caught the early rac call around 6 o'clock and headed out to the track field for my usual routine jog. While I had begun stretching and preparing to take off, I was approached by what appeared to be a fellow jogger until I glanced up and tried to identify him to no avail. I've seen every inmate on the compound at least once and I never forget a face. But this guy, I had never seen in my life. Immediately I became alive and alert. It was early morn and the sky was still a little dark but I could make out his face, he was a white man with hard looking eyes. Definitely not a casual visit, he was preparing for an attack and I had no other choice but to switch into beast mode for survival. As he advanced on me, I was prepared to rip this white man to threads. Then I saw the blade glisten like shinny jewelry from his hand as I searched his face for intent. In that instant, I knew how I would counterattack. I sized him up, I was much bigger than him and there was no way I would go out like this. This would not be an easy task for him. The whole murder scene played in my mind like a classic John Grisham crime novel but I would certainly not be the victim, I had too much to lose. So fixated on the stranger before me, what I hadn't anticipated was the dark figure gaining ground on me from behind. Where in the hell did he come from? Like a theft in the night, he snuck up on me. I never saw him, I felt him; the power from the savage thrust to my spine with a sharp object. The shock, the paralyzing pain nearly took my breath away as the driving force behind the knife plunged into me, thrust after thrust; digging into my wounded flesh like a blood thirsty villain. I lost count after the fifth hit. Apparently, someone wanted me dead... So on the cold pavement; there I lie immersed in my own life's blood while gazing up at the early morning sky, slipping in and out of consciousness.

It was nothing less than a miracle that I survived that incident. I was gutted eight times and lost an excessive amount of blood, along with nearly thirty pounds. Yes, I caught a raw deal, but by the Mercy and grace of Allah, I was spared to see another day. Obviously, I'd been doing something right. In the intensive care unit where I would spend the next four months trying to recover from my near death experience, I struggled with depression and extreme paranoia of my enemies coming back to finish me off. I was hurt and helpless and unable to defend myself. Then one night while laying in my bed, wrangling with inner demons, the voice of my spiritual father,

Minister FM came through the darkness of my mind saying these words. "Did not you think that you wouldn't be tried for that which you claim you believe? Who are you to fear man as you should fear Allah...Who was it that raised you from death....Brother let Allah deal with your enemies, they planned, but Allah is the best of planners"

I wept and prayed after that experience, asking Allah's forgiveness for my lack of faith. Though I allowed my emotions to subdue me momentarily, never once did I curse or question Allah for what he'd permitted to happen to me. I knew that if I could just clear up the fog in my head long enough to focus then the wisdom in it would soon manifest. I knew that in every so called problem, there was opportunity for good to come forth like a beautiful flower in spring time. So patiently, I waited for my sunshine to come. And when I was finally discharged from the hospital and placed back in population, the news came to me. Alfonzo, an orderly working down in RND was one of the first faces I encountered as I was brought back to the facility. RND was a processing building that all inmates had to go to before being placed on the compound.

Alfonzo expressed his concern and said that he was happy to see me back. Then as he was about to make his exit, he congratulated me on the success of RISING SUN. Now this left me in a puzzled state. I hadn't heard form Eddie, or any of the members since my fall. I wasn't sure if I still had an organization, though I prayed and hoped that Eddie and the others were confident enough to move on without me. I knew there were some forces who prayed for our downfall, which was why I had been struck down, figuring that if they took the head, then the body would automatically collapse. Little did they know that someone much more powerful than I was acting as Commander and Chief and I...Well I was just a mere servant, and a proud one at that. Back on the compound amongst all my fellow inmates, I learned that not only did I still have an organization, but RISING SUN had increased to almost a staggering eighty members strong while I was gone. I couldn't believe it. The moment the word got out that I was back, Eddie rounded every one up and led the pack down to the rac yard. Upon my arrival and seeing this demonstration, Bloods and Crips and various other brothers from different religious backgrounds all gathered together in one group, it was like I'd died and gone to heaven. I can't adequately express how good a feeling it was to see what I had been praying about for months on, come to fruition right before my eyes. Call me soft, or whatever you may, but the sight of my brothers standing together like a solid fist, brought me to tears.

Every one of them embraced me and welcomed me back. Caught up in the moment, I couldn't help from reflecting over some of my father's lectures. How Allah had ordained for us to struggle and that hardship was attached to everything that was of value. But after the difficulty, ease would surely come. So it took for me to tangle with death in order for my dreams to transform into a reality. Allah is definitely the best of planners! Would I go under the knife again to see my brothers unite? I would do it without hesitation because the idea of unification amongst the gang members and brothers in general, was much greater than my little life. And it was more than evident, that my tragedy was the apex, in which compelled these brothers to step up in my absence. But of course, there was more to it. With difficulty come ease and then another difficulty. Once you jump one hurtle, there's always another. During our discussion, I was informed that while I was away, there had been lots of tension brewing between some of my newest members and the Islam Nation.

The rumor inside the prison was that the Brotherhood was responsible for my stabbing. Many felt that it was behind the launching of my own organization that drew envy from amongst my brothers. To make it even more convincing is the fact that, four IN members had been thrown into solitary and put under investigation the following morning of my accident. I knew nothing of this. As I was being told this ridiculous story, I actually didn't consider the seriousness of it until some of the gang members within RISING SUN began urging me to give them the green light to go at the Islam Nation brothers. The Bloods and Crips together said that it would've been handled already, but they didn't want to make such a move without my approval. I couldn't believe what I was hearing, couldn't believe the predicament I had been placed in. Such absurdity had never even entered my mind. I was reliving a page right out of the history books. The mysterious white face on the track that morning was forever engraved in my mind. I had always thought that maybe my death attempt was a result of something I said during my lecture. Possibly some of the white gangs may have taken offense to my call for unity amongst my own kind and decided to put me in the side pocket. But I doubt if they'd even have the guts to pull something like that off, considering the consequences of a possible racial war. It was so confusing to me.

In all truth, I didn't know who tried to off me but I was certain of one thing though and that was, we damn sure weren't gonna start shedding each other's blood. RISING SUN was about love, peace and unity amongst one another. I had to explain to the gang members of the history old deceitful tactics of the Government to divide people up and conquer them. I told them that what happened to me was undoubtedly a blessing in disguise. It is because of my accident that you all are standing before me, once rivals, but now brothers of the same struggle. Now that we are together, it's time to build, not destroy. And the first order of business was to settle any disputes between RISING SUN and the Brotherhood and from there, work like hell for the release of the four Islam Nation soldiers who'd been falsely apprehended. Unfortunately my friend and mentor Rodney X was one of the four locked down, which made my job a little harder. So along with three of my comrades who stayed by my side like a mobile phone, we proceeded on our way to smooth out any rough edges with the Brotherhood. I could feel the mounting tension all around us in our travels to seek out our brothers and make amends. Many anticipated drama; they wanted war instead of peace. But war with us, wasn't gonna happen, at least not on my watch.

On the rac yard that very same day, a meeting took place after the four o'clock count between us and members of the Islam Nation. We discussed a number of different issues. At the top of the list, was getting rid of all the bad blood between us. Once that was established, the next subject was us working together. The gang members in RISING SUN all got a chance to speak their minds. Their main concern was ensuring that what happen to me, never happen again. It was more than obvious that there were unseen forces that would rather see us busting each other's heads like savages then to see us unified together and acting civilized. Their own wickedness back fired on them. Instead of war erupting, peace was established on that historical day. Only ALLAH could be the author of something so magnificent.

From that day forward, we were a force to be reckoned with on the compound. It soon got to the point where we started conducting the self improvement classes on the rac yard because the Chapel Department wasn't big enough to hold us. We studied together and we had the largest PT class on the compound. Those who didn't have their GED were required to get it. We tutored the brothers who needed help. Many of them read on a third grade level. But we had a solution for that because if there was one brother who couldn't read then that was one too many. The most touching moments for me was watching the gang members striving to make a change. I had Bloods and Crips united under RISING SUN. The sleeping giants were finally beginning to awaken. They were now seeing that they'd been brothers all the time. Of course, there were still many who weren't quite ready to make that transition. But I was optimistic. It was only a matter of time.

Those who had joined onto RISING SUN expressed to me that they had simply grown tired of the lifestyle that they were living. Nothing good would ever come of it and everyday on the streets, a family member or close homey were getting shot down by someone who looked just like them. They respected the stance I made to try and bring peace between them. In a group like session, these brothers declared to me that it was my sacrifice, my willingness to risk my life to see them (Bloods and Crips) come together, is what finalized their decision to commit themselves to RISING SUN in my absence. Each member embraced me, said they loved me and promised to protect me from any future attacks. Their loyalty to me was unquestionable. They didn't let me out of their sight. Wherever I went, there would be at least three or four brothers by my side. At the break of dawn, when I'd go out for my morning jog, my comrades would be right there waiting on the track until I finished. Of course, I didn't believe all the security was necessary, I even refused it in the beginning but these brothers wouldn't budge, insisting that we take precautions. But the more I began to analyze the situation, the more sense it started to make.

Nothing of this magnitude had ever been done before. Well, with the exception of OG big homey, Stanley Tookey Williams trying to bring the two communities together, but we saw firsthand what the Terminator did with the Peacemaker. And it definitely didn't help being behind enemy lines. However, I believe that God had his hand in this because it seemed like out of nowhere, RISING SUN started to take on a life of its own. Thanks to our prison reform Brother Minister, John Muhammad who personally informed the staff at the Call Now newspaper of the tremendous progress we were making here inside the prison, news about the organization began to kick off. At the editor's request, I wrote to her giving her an in-depth account of how RISING SUN came into being. I told her about the revelation to start my own organization, being revealed to me through several recurring dreams, as well as my assassination attempt. Along with that information, I sent pictures of reformed RISING SUN gangbangers. In the next Call Now issue, there was our picture, following a full page article on us. At the top of the page, the headliner read "After Difficulty, Comes Ease" then it went on to talk about how my near death experience sparked a movement that united majority of the gangbangers in both Bloods and Crips communities at the prison. It was such a beautiful and well informed article.

That was a very emotional time for me, particularly because I could see and feel Allah empowering me and raising me up to a level beyond my comprehension. From that one article alone, we received a considerable amount of press from well wishers, other black owned newspapers who desired to know more about RISING SUN. Letters began to pour in from incarcerated brothers and sisters around the country who were in support of the movement. Many of them were gang-bangers wanting to know the organizations ideology, so that they could possibly attempt to add more Chapters at their present location reflecting the same principles. The feedback we were getting was unbelievable. Eddie and I definitely had our job cut out for us. We had to respond to tons of mail, in which we would include inside, the entire layout of RISING SUN's program. Progress was moving fast and this motivated us all to push even harder. Rodney X and the others were released around this time, after months of paper work and pressuring the administration. Everything was going so well, we just knew that trouble was under way. Evil pursuers had tried to destabilize RISING SUN in its infancy stages but had failed. I wasn't so naïve to think that the trial was over; in fact it had just begun. But now that the spotlight was on us, thousands of concerned supporters writing to us weekly, mentions of RISING SUN in Jet, as well as Essence magazine, they couldn't just handle us any kind of way.

The idea to unite the Bloods and Crips was an idea whose time had come and there wasn't a force strong enough to stop this vision from growing into its full potential. Lots of people wanted to see this happen. Even a few celebrities whom I won't mention by name at this time, sent me some words of encouragement and offered their assistance if I should ever need it. With all the beautiful people coming into our lives, none was more exciting to me as Ms. Prina Carrington. A thriving journalist out of the Washington DC area, but originally from Richmond Virginia, she wrote to me one day out of the blue after following our story by way of the Call Now newspaper, as well as several other periodicals who'd been covering our progress from the beginning. In her address, she commended me on our success indicating that she wrote weekly columns for the Washington Post. Aside from the work she did for the newspaper, she also informed me that she'd earned her bachelor's degree in sociology and that she shared a keen interest in any movement whose aim was to improve the community. Ms. Carrington wanted an exclusive interview. I was excited to say the least. Not necessarily because of the extra exposure RISING SUN would get, but I hadn't been around a woman in over a decade. And to make matters even worse, she was dangerously gorgeous. Underneath of each news column she wrote for the Washington Post was a lovely photo of her. She was even more stunning in person.

At about 5' 9" in height, she had the smoothest, butter milk brown skin I'd ever seen. She was the embodiment of beauty, definitely model potential. And to compliment all of that, she was intellectually brilliant. In the beginning of our dialogue, I'm embarrassed to admit that I was a bit intimidated by her strong presence, but she had a way of making a brother feel relaxed. During our conversations, I would soon learn that on her long list of clients of whom she'd written columns on over the years, was my favorite author, "The Ghost". This news totally blew me away. Personally, I didn't know him but I loved this talented brother. He was the truth, simply put. I had every book of his that had ever been published. One afternoon while the beautiful journalist and I were visiting, I asked her if she could get me an autograph copy of the author's next novel. "Why don't you call and ask him yourself," she said to me. Of course, I took her response to be a joke.

"Are you serious?" I asked. Ms. Carrington was not only serious about me calling the author personally but she went on to tell me that she'd spoken to him in length about the possibility of him writing my autobiography. My favorite author wanted to write about my life. Could my luck get any better? An old folk saying came to mind as the sister drop the news on me; 'that if you would take one step towards God, then he'd take two towards you.' And that was real talk because the blessings were coming so fast that it was almost unreal.

Ms. Carrington got the exclusive interview she wanted and as a result, she printed a wonderful article about RISING SUN in the Washington Post newspaper. This thing was getting so big that I had to seek legal representation to ensure that the name, RISING SUN was secured and of course to legitimize my organization. With the lady journalist helping us, we were able to set up a website for the organization as well as my own personal my space, face book and twitter pages. In many cities and states across the country, request from gang bangers were pouring in, asking for my permission to use RISING SUN as a base to start their own Chapters. But this I had to be careful of. There was a process that had to take place before I could just allow anyone to jump on the RISING SUN bandwagon.

Brothers and sisters had to be screened, undergoing certain qualifications before they could even be considered to handle such a position as representing the organization. So by way of the internet and email, we sent out instructions for all who was interested.

Meanwhile, I was in discussion with the "The Ghost" about him writing the autobiography. I was actually honored to have him of all authors to do this. For starters, I was fascinated by his unique style of writing and most importantly, we both shared that same revolutionary spirit, which could easily be felt by exploring his writing. I was so grateful to Allah for all the great people coming into my life, particularly the lovely Ms. Carrington. I mean this sister was really going out of her way to help turn the organization into a success. She went from writing columns on us, to doing secretarial work for free. She informed me of the numerous Government Grants available for us to assist in the building of different programs we might implement under the organization. She was amazing, the ideas she brought to the table were simply brilliant and I could see her quickly becoming a team player. To me, she was more than just a journalist hard up for good news worthy stories but she seemed to have this certain passion about her work. I didn't understand it at first then one early Saturday morning, I received a surprised visit from her. Because of the far distance she had to travel to see me, I only saw her once every two months, twice if I was lucky. But on this particular occasion, she'd already been down that previous week and was back again. She was a joy to be around and I really valued her friendship but truthfully, I struggled like hell to contain the beast inside me. It was literally like torture to be in the presence of such a beauty and maintain decent business oriented conversation. One time during our visit, she was speaking so passionately about the potential and success that RISING SUN could have, that I stopped her in mid sentence.

I looked deeply into those attractive eyes of hers and very politely, I said, "Ms Carrington, you're a journalist. You write for one of the most prestigious newspapers in the country. I'm curious...tell me why is RISING SUN so important to you? Why do you even care to write about a bunch of gangbangers uniting? I just don't get it," I said lastly and then I drank from the bottle water she got me from the vending machine. After a long pause, Ms. Carrington went on to reveal to me that her eighteen year old son was heavily into the streets currently living in Richmond, Virginia. He was up to his neck in drugs and crime and that she was terrified that if he continued on that destructive path, he'd end up just another statistic. I saw a different Ms. Carrington that day. Not a professional, but a vulnerable concerned mother who wanted to save her only child from the streets. What was most shocking to me was the fact that her son had attended Muhammad University from second grade on up to Junior High School, which was very impressive to me and puzzling at the same time. She told me that in spite of her many sacrifices to shelter him and ensure that he get the best schooling, her efforts only seemed to have been in vain, considering the life he chose. Counselors at MUI detected early signs of behavior problems, which perhaps were the result of the devastating homicide of his father when he was just a young boy, so says the family therapist. Admittedly, the journalist claimed that no one could seem to reach him, adding that she'd just about given up hope until she met me. She said the moment she heard of RISING SUN, she made it a point to seek out the person responsible for such an idea. Then not too long afterwards, she drops the bomb on me.

Almost on the brink of tears, this beautiful sister pleaded with me to help her save her child…Damn…And to think that I had it all figured out. What a hell of a predicament to be put in, I mean this was the ultimate test for me. And although at that particular moment of silence as I hurriedly tried to recover from her unexpected request to help her son, I knew that I'd do everything within my power to assist her. I knew without a shadow of a doubt that I'd go all out for this woman. Because in those tired eyes of hers, what I saw was the unconditional love and pains of every weary stricken, black mother who didn't want to see their sons slaughtered in the streets like mere cattle and carried off to an early grave. She wanted me to reach out to Doug Jr. and try to convince him to give up the street life in exchange for becoming a member of RISING SUN.

After agreeing to help her, Ms. Carrington promised to do whatever it took to make this thing work even if it meant moving back to the city of Richmond and starting a Chapter there. Now this I was not expecting. This sister was willing to give up her life, accomplishments that had taken her years upon years to acquire, all to attempt to save her boy. That was indeed real, genuine love. I had a real soft spot for the journalist. You couldn't help but admire a woman of her caliber. But I had to exercise self control for the sake of handling RISING SUN business. So she put me in touch with her son, Doug and I started by writing a letter to him. In that correspondence, I laid out the organizations aims and purposes, as well as giving him a run down on where he could fit in. What I knew from experience is that, a lot of these street cats didn't want to sell drugs. They were products of their hopeless environments where drug sells and vicious gun play was the rule of the day. A place where positive role models were very few, which left the budding youth little or no options to do something productive with their lives. Drugs and gangs were now the number one employer in our community. Being a willing participant in that same life, born and raised up in those same slums, no one understood this concept more than me.

I became my environment, a neighborhood submerged with hustlers and gangsters, distributing death to my own while in the same process giving birth to a whole new generation of potential criminals. So when I came at Doug, I didn't come condemning him like many of our elders would do. Hell no because I understand that there is a cause to every effect. Doug's actions were in fact the effect of a cause that he had yet to discover. And my job was to disclose to him that valuable information. I wanted to first establish a bond like friendship with the youngster and set his mind at ease in hopes to open the door for the more serious talks. I didn't expect a miracle. I knew he was caught up in the streets therefore, I wasn't really looking for him to grasp all the information I was hitting him with, particularly because to a lot of the youth around his age, it was in a sense foreign to them. But to my surprise, the brother not only read my thoughts, but he began writing me these incredible letters that were full of inspiration. He admitted that he liked the whole concept of an organization set up strictly for the unification of gangs; however his only hang up was giving up his only source of income. What would he do for money if he gave up selling drugs? This was a question I got on many occasions from brothers who was interested in learning about the organization. I would say to these guys, look man, it's a million hustles, why settle for one? You mean to tell me with all the billions of black dollars that contribute to the American economy; we can't create a product other than drugs to sell to our people. For instance, in the prison where I was currently serving time, brothers who had joined on to RISING SUN, but particularly those who were dealing in drugs, had to restrain from their ways and earn their money doing something productive. So to compensate, we set up classes where we'd teach brothers how to crochet everything from Home Tradition Afghans to stuff animals, scarf's and baby blankets. This was a very popular profession in prison where if brothers took it seriously, they could make good money. Just ask Martha Steward. I jolted down some of my business plans and sent them to Doug, encouraging him to take a portion of that drug money and invest in one of the plans that best suited him. I told him straight up that he was playing in a game where the cards had already been set for him to lose, and that death awaited him or a lengthy prison sentence if he didn't seize this opportunity being presented before him. Then to support my claims, I'd always send him little excerpts from out of the Call Now newspaper where Minister FM gave the break down on how our Government was secretly plotting to exterminate us under the bogus Anti Gang Unit.

In a critical time such as this, candy coating reality would only be a disservice to Doug. After about a month of correspondence back and forth through letters, at his request, I mailed him a visitation form. Evidently, our telephone conversations and letters proved to be affective because even his mother divulged the fact that she could see him slowly changing. His calls to her became more frequent and the discussions, she says were becoming more and more positive. I got a letter in the mail from Ms. Carrington about one month later, indicating that she was making arrangements to relocate back to her place of birth, (Richmond, Virginia.) She wanted my permission to jump start our very first Chapter down in that area. When I first read that part of the letter, I thought to myself, man this thing is really happening. This woman was undoubtedly heaven sent and I felt so blessed to have her on my side. A goddess she was, the kind of woman every noble-man needed by his side. I didn't hesitate in getting back at her and giving her my blessing, along with every necessary resource that was needed for her to make this dream of mine a reality. And the beauty of it all was that she wasn't alone in Richmond Virginia, there was a major support system already in place to assist her in building the movement.

Meanwhile with Ms. Carrington pushing our program on the outside, it gave us the motivation to thrive even harder inside the prison. There were so many unresolved issues pertaining to the unfair treatment of prisoners that we as a community needed to come together and address. For starters, the environment in which we lived was unfit for any human being to be doing long periods of time. The food was terrible, I mean the list of disparities went on and on, and unless a courageous spirit rose up against the opposition, these people would just continue to walk over us, they needed to be taught a lesson. I had this explosive idea in my head. It was brilliant actually but at the same time, it was dangerous as hell. This thing was so risky that for two whole months, I did nothing but think it over, weighing out my options, the pros and cons and consequences that would possibly follow as a result of my actions.

Neither looked promising but finally I had come to the conclusion that I could no longer sit idly by, watching as this administration handled us unjust without cause. Before speaking a word to my comrades about my plans, I sent a message to my journalist friend, indicating my urgency to see her at her earliest convenience. The telephone along with all outgoing mail was subject to be monitored, mines imparticular, which left us with only one option. That following Saturday morning she was there waiting in the visiting room looking as lovely as I had ever seen her. She'd traded in her conservative apparels for a pair of fitting blue jeans and some cute heels that enhanced her height by a few inches. There's nothing more appealing to me than the sight of a naturally beautiful woman. She had a set of jet white, perfect teeth and her lips were full and luscious looking. Impeccable golden brown skin with no blemishes and her hair was cut short and styled similar to my fantasy dream girl, Nia Long. That morning for nearly one hour, I sat mesmerized, admiring the beauty before me while listening to her rave on and on about the growing support for our movement. Influential names like Tavis Smiley were speaking out positively about the organization. Many folks from all walks of life could relate to what RISING SUN was about because if not directly affected, then indirectly, we all suffered in one way or another from the mounting gang violence around the country.

Crime wasn't restricted to one particular ethnic group, nor a certain skin color, but this thing was real as though it had taken on its own life form. As I began to give her the run down about my plans to initiate a "Black Out" within the prison, she suddenly scoots over closer to me and out of nowhere she hits me with a soft, breath taking kiss that leaves a brother speechless. While in the process of trying to bounce back from her unexpected knockout punch, she smiled at me with those clear, direct, and penetrating brown eyes then strangely, she thanked me.

"For what Ms. Carrington," I quickly replied somewhat puzzled.

"You can call me, Prina," she insisted with a warm and engaging smile. She suddenly took one of my hands in hers. Damn...it seemed like it had been ages since I'd last had the pleasure of being this close to a lovely woman. With her gently caressing my hand, slowly stroking each finger one after the other, I tussled with my emotions like a battered soldier fending for his life against a treacherous enemy. God, I just wanted to hold her adorable little frame in my arms forever. I wanted to put my hands to her face and kiss the corner of her mouth. I wanted.... so much for my sexual appetite.

I had to get a grip on myself... and I did. Prina continued. She went on to say that RISING SUN had given her life a whole new profound purpose and that because I had intervened on her son's behalf, there was hope for him. The organization was a safe haven for him and a host of other young hopeless indolence's who were tangled up in the spider web of illusion and endless deception. The mother and son team were partnering up to start a Chapter in Richmond Virginia. The ball was beginning to roll and Prina had already put in her transfer from her job at the DC newspaper. She had impeccable credentials and a relentless track record as one of the most persistent and hard working journalists around, so landing another gig wouldn't be a problem. Furthermore, we needed a platform to let the world know about the organization and what better way to promote it then through Prina's news columns.

Speaking of which, the "Black Out". Originally, this was what I had summoned the journalist down to the prison to talk about but we got off track somehow...As I stated earlier, the prison administration needed to be taught a valuable lesson. See, unlike many of my prison peers, I understand that the prison industrial system is in fact the new plantation and the 'inmate' is simply another name for slave. So with that in mind, it's only logical to assume that, because of the above mentioned, we as "so called inmates" is not deserving of a descent living quarters. Often times, our food would be out dated and even spoiled in some instances, scraps off the table that weren't even edible for public consumption.

We were out cast to them, animals...inmates and slaves. The whole scene was just downright despicable. Men stacked on top of men with piss infected urinals parked right beside the bed. It reminds me of the Trans Atlantic slave ship that brought our ancestors over here. It was a cest pool for nasty germs, so you can imagine how rampant diseases spread throughout the prison. Then to make matters even worse, the budget given to the bureau by the DEPT OF JUSTICE to improve and maintain living conditions around the prison, wasn't being allocated properly and as a result; who do you think suffered? For this reason alone, I was gonna call for a "Black Out". A food strike, no work, cut out education and even sports. We would cease to participate in all BOP operation until our concerns got addressed. An idea as extreme as this may seem a bit ridiculous to some, considering the disunity amongst the prisoners and simply black folks in general, but I knew the power of unity and in spite of the diversity and false barriers that kept us at odds with one another, we all had one thing in common. We were all chained and locked down with distinctive numbers. Whether black or white, brown, red, or yellow, we were feeling the heat, living under such mind altering conditions. So the "Black Out" wasn't about just black brothers, but all brothers. The whites, Latinas, Mexicans, had to be involved in order for this thing to be effective.

I would appeal to them all. There would be repercussions of course and those who took part in this courageous act, I would strongly encourage them to honker down and stock up on commissary, because an institution lock down was inevitable. It would get real nasty but as long as we remained defiant and gelled together like a solid fist, we'd eventually prevail. They would come for whom ever the "TROUBLE MAKER" was...Me. Some weakling would sooner or later jump ship and finger me out. And the goon squad would be there in a flash to snatch me up. Initially, it's a move I anticipated, which is where Prina's role would become most helpful. Already, there had been one attempt on my life for something far less than what I was about to do, so typically I expected opposition. The million dollar question was in what fallacious disguise this opposition would manifest itself. Never the less, if Ms. Prina followed instructions well, when and if the goons came, they'd most surely have to tread very lightly and be extra careful in how they handled me. I told her to shine the spotlight on the institution. Put it on blast and let the world know about the **"Black Out"** and the inhumane treatment of prisoners, in which compelled us to take this course of action. And don't worry too much about me, I assured the lovely journalist upon observing a hint of worry coursing the lining in her face. Whatever happens as a result of my actions is okay. If they take my body, my last breath then so be it, but rest assured that the idea of RISING SUN would live on because the seed of peace has already been planted. There was no turning back now… "And Prina," I said extracting her full and undivided attention. "I'm counting on you. I need you to pool every resource you have in alerting the people to what's happening in here. You don't have to look any further than yourself. We have everything we need."

"Yes, I know what needs to be done." she assured. Ten minutes left before our wonderful visit was to be over, the end always sucked! It was nothing but pure torment to watch her depart from my life, though it was only momentarily. I had been actually imagining the pathetic images (her leaving) when her softness suddenly snuggled up against me, laying her head gently on my shoulder. Following her lead, I sheltered her in my arms, caring nothing of the piercing eyed officers present. As I began planting a trail of soft kisses along her forehead….her cheek, it was then that I noticed what appeared to be tears glistening down her ebony cheeks. I can't even express the displeasure I get in seeing a woman's tears. Without even giving it a second thought, I lifted her hand to my lips for a kiss.

"Hey you, what's all that for. You alright…."

"Yes I'm okay…Laughs, "I am so sorry. I don't know what the hell just came over me."

"Don't apologize," I said with a smile as I wiped away the dampness from her face. "Is something going on that I should know about?"

"No, of course not."

"Then what's with the tears," I state and gaze deeply into her eyes."

"Trust me, you don't wanna know," says Prina.

"They gonna end our visit any minute, don't leave a brother in suspense like this."

Her lovely smile suddenly disappeared as her eyes came to set dead on mine. Prina told me that she didn't understand how it had happened, but she was falling for me. She said that her tears had stem from the painful thought of having to continue leaving the prison without me...Damn, she was right; I didn't need to hear that. Not now, not with only minutes left before the end of our visit. What about my feelings? What about the love and admiration that I'd been harboring inside me ever since the very first moment I laid eyes on her. As visitors were being ushered out, staring in a trance at this remarkable woman wave goodbye, I wondered did she even know that her coming into my life was a prayer that I'd been praying for a very long time...I wondered also as I caught the kiss she blew, would I ever have the opportunity to see that pretty face again. And if so, when...Little did I know, it wouldn't be any time soon.

Chapter

2

Nat Turner

After the visit was finally over and done with, it was back to my dismal reality where I retired to my cell, made prayer and meditated for nearly an hour over how I'd approach this new situation, (The Black Out). Now that Prina was informed, I felt comfortable enough to discuss my plans with the rest of the members. Understand that many before me had attempted to do this, but had failed at it due to improper preparation. In every organization, there was a potential traitor amongst the Brotherhood, slithering on his belly like a poisonous snake waiting for the perfect opportunity to strike. So I knew that the moment I unleashed this idea, I'd have to move faster than the speed of light before the mighty hand of the administration made an attempt to neutralize our movement. One careless move could compromise everything; therefore, it was absolutely imperative that I took calculated steps. I was wrecking my brain trying to figure out my first approach when Eddie, my Chief Aid, rushed into the cell alerting me of a brawl in action between a couple rival gang bangers. Within a matter of minutes, it was over as a pack of uniformed officers intervened. Standing there with a few comrades of mine, observing the uniforms attempt to remove the trouble makers from the housing unit, it suddenly came to me that from that spectacle, I'd found the missing piece to my puzzle. Before now, I had not the slightest idea of what tactic I'd use to bring brothers together under the watchful eye of the prison guards without arousing their suspicion.

An opportunity like this would never present itself again, which was why I had to seize the moment. Normally, in the streets, Los Angeles to be specific, where Bloods and Crips were most prevalent, they were bashing each other's heads in at will, but ironically when they entered the Federal prison system, thousands of miles from home where their members were significantly small, compared to other various gangs, in many cases they were forced to unite to protect themselves. But even that new found Brotherhood didn't stop these guys from locking necks like a pair of raging pit-bulls. Nevertheless, the incident would serve as my excuse to get a meeting authorized by SIS to "squash the beef". SIS (Special Investigative Services) was to us in Federal Prison, what the Alphabet Boy's (FBI) were to those in free society. I met with the Bloods and Crips and we spoke in length about what went down with the fight, which was nothing more than a foolish misunderstanding. It was nothing. I gave them the spill on how I planned to use that particular situation to get everyone together. They were with me one hundred percent. With their permission, I immediately started putting my plan into motion. RISING SUN disseminated out onto the compound, moving discreetly as humanly possible and in an orderly fashion.

Meanwhile, I went to work on Simmons, the head SIS officer. Being an investigator and all, this guy was well aware of my influence inside the prison and as well as my reputation as a peace maker. So when I described the brewing tension bubbling between the two groups as a result of that fight, my words didn't fall on deaf ears. I painted a horrible picture for him of a mob of angry men spewing hatred; knifing and carving at each other with such intensity, that it would make the works of a butcher in a meat market seem like child's play.

"Surely, sir you want nothing like that to go down on your watch. And me personally, I don't wanna see my brothers hurt one another. If we can prevent it, Mr. Simmons, I'm at your service." Of course he wanted to avoid a prison war. Violence was bad for everyone, the administration, as well as the inmate population. So he granted my request, asked me what I needed and I told him...

One by one, I along with brothers from RISING SUN made rounds to spread the word about the meeting. I caught static from some of my brothers because of my plans to include the white gangs, the (Arian Brotherhood and Dirty White Boys.) A lot of my comrades failed to see the bigger picture. This wasn't about the (AB's) feelings towards us or blacks in general, nor was it about our personal feelings towards them. It was about all of us receiving the same unfair treatment. And that alone should be reason enough for us to unite and fight this administration. Plus, I heard somewhere once that men chained together were brothers anyhow. A representative for the Arian Brotherhood, Big Mike found that statement amusing when he, myself and a mutual friend had our sat down. Like many, he'd been misinformed in his thinking that the Islam Nation was a group of black, radical racist. And because of my affiliations with the IN, I too was a hater of the white race. He couldn't have been further from the truth.

I gave him a bit of enlightenment, but I didn't want to get into a long and drawn out discussion about race. Later for that, the **Blackout** was top priority. At the end of our meeting, Big Mike still hadn't come to a decision of whether or not he'd participate, he just said he'd think about it. But he didn't say he wouldn't...For the most part, brothers weren't as objective as I'd figured they'd be. Judging from the positive responses we were receiving; it was obvious to me that many shared our desire to improve the pathetic situation around us. The timing was right and definitely, we were in the right setting for a movement such as this. The U.S.P (Federal Pen) didn't have a great amount of short timers; instead there were cats in the prison with so much time that they had letters in the place of numbers (Lifers). With nowhere to go and nothing to lose, what the hell was a couple weeks or a month on lock down to these dudes. I had just about covered everyone of whom I thought would make this thing work...Well with one exception. The Mexicans were a different story. Due to their extracurricular activities and the fact that many of them lived better lives inside the wall than on the streets, they wouldn't dare do anything to disrupt that comfort. The groups inside the prison were segregated, the Mexicans more so than the others. We were considered outsiders to them. Plus they had their hands into everything illegal and their participation would just slow up their cash flow...An ex-gangbanger who was now a member of RISING SUN, warned me against approaching the Mexicans. He said in prison they acted one way, but on the streets of LA, it was open season on blacks. Every day, he said brothers and sisters and small children were being slaughtered by the hands of the Mexican Mafia.

The meeting had a major turn out. There on the enormous soccer field, just about every black and Latina gang as well as regular supporters showed up to hear what we had to say.

Among us was the head or representative of these distin-
guished organizations. To invite out every member of each
gang would be straight up foolish, not to mention risky.
Everyone received instruction; the entire layout of what the
meeting was all about. No one objected to the fact that in order
for change to occur, it would take brothers standing together
in solidarity. The information was relayed to each representative then in return; they were to go on back to their respective
members with instructions. The prison officials watched the
huddle from a distance, but they never bothered us. They
were informed from on high that the large crowd was a peace
rally and not to interrupt unless they spotted something
unusual. But all they saw was a peaceful gathering, a host of
brothers of all hues and various shades posted up in congregation attempting to establish unity. But unbeknownst to the
officers on duty and the entire administration, we were
launching the first stage of engagement.

The warden made his rounds once a week. He was a snob-
by redneck fella with a huge pop belly and stank attitude. You
know the type, one who thought that rank was important and
showed contempt for those he regarded as beneath him. That
following Tuesday afternoon at lunch time, as the warden
along with a host of staff and other personnel were posted up
in the center of the dining hall, masquerading like they were
thoroughly concerned about the needs of their prisoners, they
got the shock of a lifetime.

Nearly three to four hundred brothers bombarded the
dining hall that day, holding in their hands a COPE OUT
form, (Grievances) addressed exclusively to the warden
himself. Nothing of this magnitude had ever happen before;
men coming together in record numbers to demand from the

administration, respect, healthy, nutritious food, served to us from the prison's dining hall. Every month it seemed as though the items on the commissary list increased by a few cents. We were charged a fee just to speak to medical personnel about a health related issue…But even a child will act out and run over top of you if you allow it. And in the case of the administration, they were only doing what we allowed them to do. We had been laying down for too long, content in our misery, a door mat for officials to walk on. But no more…the tension was thick and on the faces of every officer in that kitchen was a look of anxiety, skepticism…I was to later learn that the Arian Brotherhood had participated in the dining hall spectacle but even more surprising and amazing to me at the same time, was to hear that two notorious Mexican gangs had joined the fight. Obviously, I had misjudged these brothers. Through the wire, it was said that the Arian Brotherhood had a hand in their coming aboard. But who in the hell cared about that, they were on the team, which was most important to me. To witness all these rival groups moving in sync, I'm certain this put the administration on high alert. For the next few days, the compound would be full of gossip about what happen. But as I had expected, with the passing of time, doubt about the seriousness of our concerns began to seep into the minds of the warden, as well as the employees under him.

The officers made jokes about it. The move we made was labeled by prison officials as a *Fabricated Civil Rights Movement.* Real life comedians, right. Already anticipating their reluctance to respond positively to our request in a timely fashion, we struck again two weeks later inside the dining hall, but this time our numbers had nearly doubled. RISING SUN had been making rounds and putting in serious foot work after the first incident. We had to follow this thing all the way through if we expected to see real results. So we went around the compound pressing the brothers, encouraging patience and making sure that everyone remained focus and not get discouraged. It paid off. The Warden was so pissed to see us back, that his pale skin became so red and his face so distorted that I thought he'd catch on fire right there in the middle of the dining hall. I mean, the ruthless redneck in him began to seep from out of his pores. Then suddenly, the rosy cheek warden snarled at the officers present, demanding that they disallow any further inmates to approach him. He declined to address any of our concerns, nor would he accept anymore grievances. For one split second, we saw the fear leap off the warden's face at the sight of us. He'd never looked so vulnerable, so unsure of himself. Nearly half of the cafeteria was there to see him. He was scared straight, every last one of them. They were all actors. The control they exercised over the inmate population was where their confidence derived from. But in that dining hall on this particular day, their confidence had been shaken. Finally, officers formed a blockade around the warden and together they left the dining hall in a hurry.

Chapter

3

Next Phase

I had my journalist friend on standby. And because the *"Blackout,"* was so sensitive a topic to discuss over an open line, I had her to inform "The Ghost" on what was happening with me. Already, we had begun discussing the plans about my autobiography for approximately two months now. I had been sending the author bits and pieces of accounts of what I can recall of my life. I was racing against time. I knew not the day, nor the hour when they would come for me, but I was certain they would. Prina and I talked just about every night over the phone. She was really starting to grow on me. I would go so far as to say that I had fallen in love with this woman. Was that at all possible? For I had never felt this way about anyone in my life, it had to be love because I could feel her in the very core of my heart. But damn, this type of thing was so unhealthy for me right now. There was no telling where I'd end up in the days to come. I'd grown accustom to hearing her sweet voice. Nevertheless, I was fully committed to the mission, as well as prepared to endure whatever reper-cussions that may come as a result of my actions.

The test would come sooner than I had expected. A little over 24 hours following the dining hall incident. I had just shut my eyes to catch some sleep when a glimmer from the officers flash light shinned into my cell. Then came, "Turner, need you at the officers station, ASAP with your ID card." I heard the click, the officer unlocking the cell. My cellmate Eddie and I were wide awake at this point, both of us knowing the time. Although the guard claimed that I was only wanted for random urine screening, of course we knew better. In all the years of being confined behind these walls, I'd never once been screened for a urine test. Well there was a first time for everything, but still...After a huge hug and some sound instruction to my Chief Aid; I departed from my cell with no intentions of ever coming back...

Down the long stretched corridor, around the corner and up the dark hall way, by passing the inmate housing unit, I came upon the officer's station. The guard escorting me, pushed the door open and said, "SIS wanna see you," he states and steps back so that I could enter. "Tell me something I don't know," I say under my breath to no one imparticular as I walk in. The door suddenly closed behind me. "Have a sit Mr. Turner?"

"What's this about Mr. Simmons," I asked before grabbing a chair across from the desk he was seated on.

"Just wanna have a word with you"

"At 2:00 in the morning."

It was obvious to me by now that something else was going down. I imagine that if my first prediction was correct (moving me from the institution) then there wouldn't be anything to discuss. "You're here, Mr. Turner...because I have a problem. And believe me when I tell you that if I have a problem, then we both have a problem. I did you a favor last week. But now, I need you to return that favor."

"Mr. Simmons I don't see how I'll be able to help you. And if I can assist you, then surely, it will depend on your problem."

"You're aware of this new situation that we have with these guys, bombarding the warden with these god damn grievances."

"Of course I know about that. But sir, by no means is that our problem. I'm a convict just like the rest."

"Yeah right Turner, I hear that but the thing is... I need your help. A name or something, whose idea was it to — ?"

Give him a name. The nerve of this black bastard, obviously he had me confused with someone else. A snitch...he was asking Nat Turner to rat. Give him a name...I was dazed. I was just about to give him a verbal ass whipping when a light bulb suddenly came on in my head. I had to quickly reshuffle my deck...At nearly two o'clock in the morning, Mr. Simmons had me snatched out of bed, hoping that I could hip him to the troublemaker responsible for putting guys up to shoving grievances down the warden's throat. Evidently, he didn't know squat, not the slightest idea that the "so called" **Head Honcho** who'd put the administration on pins and needles, was sitting right in front of him. It crossed my mind that maybe I was being played, but it didn't add up. What could be gained by it? In any movement that was in direct opposition to the power structure, from pass experience, they knew that all they needed to do was knock off the head of that movement and the body would gradually dismantle itself. Well, here I was, if they wanted me, they had me. But the problem was, as of yet, they didn't know who had instigated these brothers. I figured out real quick that I could manipulate the situation to my advantage...

"So Mr. Turner, what's it gonna be. Do me this one favor and I promise you, I won't forget....For starters, take this....."

I caught the plastic bag he tossed at me and examined the contents.

"It's over five hundred books of stamps in there; I know you can use them. I confiscated them off one of the compound bookies."

The SIS officer and I held a mutual gaze for what seemed an eternity. Here's a man who had no conscience what so ever about his actions. He didn't see me or any of us brothers as someone off the distant family tree, but as a convict criminal. He was solely dedicated to the Government, a mindless robot, is what he was. I could see the mark of the beast engraved into his forehead. My blood boiled from anger and it was the first time in years, that I actually entertained tormenting thoughts of maiming another black man. But of course, they were only thoughts. I rose to my feet and concealed the bag of stamps under my arm pit, told the SIS officer that I would get back to him and then I made my exit.

There are various reasons why one might join on to many of the gangs or religious organizations on the prison compound. A lot of brothers come in wanting to sincerely better themselves, so they'll seek refuge in whatever religious group that best suits them. On the other hand, there are those guys who have a hidden agenda. They harbor dark secrets, an evader of a turbulent past they never wants to catch up with them. The organization they join is somewhat of a safe haven...their protection. But what's done in the dark, will eventually come to light. Kevin Fisher had advanced toward RISING SUN three months after its inception. A handsome black, charismatic brother who worked hard with the rest of

us in trying to make RISING SUN a strong force to be reckoned with inside, as well as beyond the prison. He was a
soldier; at least I thought he was before stumbling upon some
very disturbing evidence pertaining to his court case. Not only
was Kevin Fisher a rat for the US Government, but even more
pathetically, was the fact that his sixty two year old mother
had recently passed away in the women's federal prison. He
and his mother got caught up in a major heroin drug ring that
spread throughout the East Coast. It was a situation where he
could've spared his mom but he didn't. The feds had nothing
on her other than her son's testimony. The bastard burned his
own mother. Her case was on file in the legal department of
the prison library for everyone to view it. But so far only a
hand few of the members knew about this coward. How could
a man who turns state on his own mother be trusted? When
the pressure got thick, we in the organization wouldn't stand a
chance.

Aside from us, no one had yet to divulge this chicken heart
because if they had, he would've never made it to the prison
compound. I along with a few others had planned to meet
with him the same morning of my discussion with the SIS
officer and pull his card and urge him to check into the (Hole)
ASAP! But plans had changed...I had something better in
mind. Simmons wanted the head of the movement, the "Insti-
gator." I would provide him with the name. If the investigator
went for it, this would buy me a couple more days, or possibly
even a whole week, which was more than enough time to start
the strike... **Blackout.**

Twenty-four hours after submitting Kevin Fisher's name to
the investigator, like clockwork, the brother was picked up
and escorted from off the compound, thrown into the (SHU)

special housing unit and placed under investigation. With him in custody, I knew that it was just a matter of time before Simmons found out that I'd played him. And if Kevin didn't break down, then surely some other snake would do me the honors. Before I started talking about the **Black Out,** I informed everyone that our main objective was to go on strike, but first we would attempt to give the warden a fair warning. Well, we did that but evidently the administration didn't take us seriously. So now, it was on to the next phase. We went to work on the compound. We were devoted soldiers with a cause. Five or ten years ago, this type of thing would have been unheard of but times were quickly changing. And I guess there was a slight part of me that agreed with the naysayers? But I didn't allow that fear to discourage me. (Faith was the substance of things hoped for, the evidence of things not seen.) My faith is what pushed me forward; although some thought what I was attempting to do was impossible. But it wasn't. We had over five hundred brothers who had given their word that they were with us.

Over six hundred of us bucked the administration. When work call was announced at 7:30 am, we all remained in the housing unit. Brothers held their ground and waited patiently for what we knew would follow... (An institutional lock down.) Normally, when something of this nature happen, officers would have to pitch in to perform the duties that inmates would usually work. I'm talking unit managers, counselors, the A W (Assistant Warden) Etc...For those who are not aware, inmates run the prison. We cook, clean and prepare the food, it's us who keep the institution up and functioning, but now these responsibilities would fall on the staff. Imagine preparing a meal for fifteen hundred men and having to serve their food to them in their cells. This would be their duty as long as we remained on lock down. Many of the officers had never done this much work in their lives. After two to three days, the staff was over worked, irritated and bickering with one another for having to do things outside of their professional field. I don't know about the others, but I got a kick out of being served by the lazy bastards. In their eyes when they would bring us our food, I could tell that they hated every minute of it. There were no more friendly gestures from them, or casual conversation as it had once been, just looks of disgust and hatred for those who they felt was to blame for their temporary discomfort.

One officer, however; stop by the cell and sparked up a conversation. This particular officer ask how long did we plan to resist and idiotic questions like, what are our reasons for the strike. Why ask why? Just look around. This wasn't a place of rehabilitation, but a warehouse not even fit for animals to live. How would you feel if it were you back here, caged in like some animal? They could never muster a response whenever I'd hit them with such a question. Then I'd say to them that until our needs are addressed and we see to our satisfaction an attempt on the administration's part to right the wrong, you all had better get used to serving us. My Chief Aid and cellmate, Eddie warned me against talking like that to the officers, especially if I didn't want to blow my cover. He said that if he didn't know any better, he would think that I was the one who had instigated this whole thing. I know my partner was right, but I was also aware of the fact that we had been on lock down for a week. I really didn't expect to be on the compound that long. I only wanted to be there long enough to plant the seed of unity and to see the strike. And after that...who knows where I'd end up.

I heard his voice in my sleep...Simmons was cursing up a storm. Since the strike had begun, I had only seen him once when he accompanied the warden's entourage on their routine walk through. We acknowledge one another, but he never showed any indication that they were on to me. Certainly, if he had known then I to would've known, period. But it had happened. The jig was finally up. Shortly after the five o'clock a.m. count, movement in the hallway, coupled with the blaring sounds of the officers radio had me, wide eyed like a fiend wired off of crack. Then I heard Simmons edgy growl loud and clear... "I want his ass up, handcuffed and in my fuckin office right now!!!"

Obviously, he was pissed. I had committed the ultimate crime. The investigator had been foolishly manipulated and humiliated by an inmate...a convict. The slave had out smarted the master on his own plantation. I knew the penalty would be a harsh one. But there was no turning back for me now. The moment I stepped foot into the officer's station where Simmons waited, handcuffed from behind, the investigator had these words to say. "You are a real smart ass, huh." With a deep sigh of frustration, he folded his arms across his puny little chest then fixated his beady eyes at me and grinned. "I can't deny that you made me look like a god-damned fool." He managed a chuckled. "That was real good Turner...real good. But you know....I'll get the last laugh, right. Of course you do. You had this thing all figured out from the start. The grievances to the warden and the meeting I authorized for you to have. It was all bullshit, wasn't it...?"

I never said a word. What the hell was there for me to say? I was busted; it was finished, so save your speech. I did what I had to do and knew it was time for them to do what they had to do. I bombed first...

"You get a good look you son-of-a bitch because you will never see this compound again. When I'm done with your monkey ass, you're gonna wish you never fucked with me...I'm gonna drag your black ass through the mud and back. Now get the fuck out of my sight."

Chapter

4

The Journey of the Unknown

I
t was time to pay the piper. I was immediately ushered to the SHU (SPECIAL HOUSING UNIT) where I was to remain until my removal from the institution. Within a couple of weeks, I was on a bus heading up north. But before leaving, the angry investigator made sure to follow through on his sinister threat by making sure my stay there was miserable as possible. In my thirteen years of being locked up, occasionally in and out of the SHU, I had never been treated so foul. Although I anticipated a hard time, the incident that really got to me...I mean really made me fume, was when this redneck bullheaded officer gave me a food tray with a nasty piece of fatback (PORK) on it. I raised holy hell! But unfortunately because I had pissed off the entire administration, my complaints fell on deaf ears. It was me against the world. As it had always been, my only place of refuge was in ALLAH. So I began to engulf myself into deep meditation and prayer and because the officers found it amusing to feed a Muslim pork, I stop eating...Next time it could possibly be poison.

Thanks to the Islam Nation program, I was used to eating one meal a day or every other day. I could actually go without any food consumption up to 72 hours, or longer if need be. While in the SHU chasing off hunger pains, it became perfect-

ly clear to me the significance behind the Islam Nation
subscribing for the followers to fast. There I was confined to a
small cell, solely dependent to eat from the enemy's hand. I
understood fully how the administration and Government felt
about me and my kind. I was stirring up the troubled waters,
creating waves and they didn't like that. Although I was at the
mercy of them, a prisoner behind the enemy's line, a power
much greater than them was running the show. I felt that as
long as I remained faithful and utilized the strict discipline
principles of the IN, I'd be alright. For every part of my being
believed that I had a mission from God Himself to do what I
was doing. But first, there was a test that I had to endure.

During my early years inside the wall, there was always
talk about the JOURNEY OF THE UNKNOWN. The expression was simply another name for what the feds termed as
Diesel Therapy. I preferred the Journey of the Unknown
because once you were put on that bus or plane, there was no
telling where you'd end up. If you were deemed as a trouble
maker like me, you'd be lucky enough to criss cross the
country. Your communication with the outside world would
suddenly come to a halt because of constantly being moved
around. You were lucky if you could squeeze a phone call and
you were able to write letters, but it was highly unlikely that
you wouldn't be there in time to receive a response. And let's
not even mention visits…forget about it.

Investigator Simmons made his word his bond. All contact
with the outside world was lost from the moment I left the
USP. When he said that he'd drag me through the mud, he
meant every word. For nine long months, I stayed in transit,
arriving at a different location every week. One week I'm
down South, the next week, I'm on a plane flying out West.

The food was terrible. And between me being a non-meat eater and fasting every other day, I shredded over 20 pounds. The journey was a rough one. My main concern over all, even more than myself, was the status of the movement. My organization, were they still moving out, or had the members been picked apart and dismantled? I had no way of knowing. I wrote letters to my journalist friend, but I was always gone from the institution before she could respond to my letters. It was frustrating as hell. Although I knew Prina was just as dedicated to the mission as I, I still often questioned her loyalty. Had she followed my instructions? Did she abort the mission? You know what they say, out of sight, out of mind? My negative thoughts could sometimes get crazy. But it was only my own insecurities bugging me out. An idle mind is the devil's workshop and I definitely had a lot of idle time on my hands. Reading became a major relief and pass time for me. It had always relaxed me, but because I had been temporarily separated from my personal property, I had to choose between old school Westerns and boring romance novels. Never the less, the reading got me through the long days. And when I wasn't reading, I'd write to Prina to keep her up to speed on my status. I had even started writing her poetry. Far from a poet, however, a woman like her could have a man doing things he wouldn't normally do. Like writing her love letters and such; I couldn't shake her, though I tried desperately. I thought of her every minute of the day...seemed that way.

This love thing was complicated....like a double edged sword. I mean don't get me wrong because love is beautiful...but damn...It was pure torture to have a woman and not be able to see, kiss and touch her....to not be able to be there to love her as God had intended. Did she share those same feelings...I wondered. I kept her in my prayer's hoping that she was still down for me...Nearly eight long and strenuous months would pass before I'd get the answers to some of those near and dear questions. I arrived at the USP in Florence Co. in mid December and was immediately placed in special housing. Because of the approaching Christmas holiday and New Year (2013), it would be the longest hold over ever. The feds didn't move too much during the holidays. This meant that I could possibly be there long enough to write and get some incoming mail. Maybe even a phone call, who knows...My cellmate in the hole, a notorious gang leader from Southside Chicago was waiting to be transferred to ADX (Maximum Security Pen). The facility was located underground; the gang leader said that the institution housed some of the most dangerous men around the country. In ADX, there was no physical contact with visitors and inmates were confined to their cells 23 hours a day with the one hour reserved for rac. All reading material, including mail was put up on a screen in their cells. Talk about control. When my cellmate was done giving me the spill on how the ADX was operated, he began inquiring about my destination. Where I'd come from, where I was headed...I told him, his guest was mines.

Diesel Therapy, huh," he states with a sly grin. I confirm with a nod and then I drop it on him. As I had started to inform him about the organization, he cut me off in mid sentence.

"Tell me you not the nigga who started the RISING SUN joint..."

I simply smiled.

"Are you Nat Turner?"

"Yeah man that's me."

With my conformation, he sprung from the bed in a burst of excitement.

"Ain't this a bitch, I just finished reading about you," he went on as he kneeled to grab from under the bunk, a stack of vibe magazines and some old newspapers that he'd manage to swindle through his inside connection in the prison. My body went limp, heart pounded in anticipation as I sat frozen, watching while my new friend scrambled to find the article. Upon laying eyes on the headliner of the editorial page of the newspaper, at the top it read, *"Lost In The System, Has Any One Seen"*…It had my whole name and down at the bottom of the page, was Prina's lovely face. As I began reading the full page article, the brother didn't understand the tears of joy that instantaneously began to leap from my eyes. I had to explain that after almost a year of silence and not being able to communicate and handle my affairs, I sort of felt as though I was dead to the world. Boy was I far from the truth. I would soon learn that this article was just one of the many articles written by the journalist on my behalf. She had done everything I'd asked her to do. According to the article, the BLACK OUT had started a chain reaction in numerous prisons throughout the country. The movement hadn't lost a step in my absence but instead, it grew wings and was now soaring.

I had a strong urgency to hear Prina's voice…to thank her and just express to her how greatly she was appreciated. Thanks to her utilizing her platform at the newspaper to spread the word about RISING SUN, supporters were suddenly springing up in various parts of the country. Never was I one to believe in foolish things such as fairy tales, but the way my vision had come to life, was sort of like one of those crazy fairy tales in a movie. But of course, I knew that it was only by the grace of God that so many people had gravitated towards the movement. It was such a brilliant idea for gangbangers to unite under one banner. My cellmate agreed that it could be good for the black community, not to mention the country. The more we politicked about the impact it could have, the more my reason for being at that particular location began to manifest. ADX, Super Max was an institution designed to house the "so called" worse of the worst. Troublemaker's like me, who in the administration eyes possessed entirely too much influence over their prisoners. Until my arrival at Florence Co, I hadn't given any thought to the slight possibility that I had maybe reached my final destination. If it was true that RISING SUN had stirred up brothers in federal prisons across the country then it made sense that I wouldn't go back to general population. And so it was, almost three months later, which marked a full year in transit, I was finally transferred to the "Super Max" where I would remain until I finished my sentence.

Chapter

5

No Place Like Home...3 ½ Years Later

There are no words to adequately express the tremendous joy I felt to reenter back into free society after being gone for so long. The world seemed to have changed drastically in sixteen years. It took some time to get adjusted but once I did, it was like I'd never left. Prina had transferred back to her place of birth (Richmond, Virginia) just as she'd promised she would. She moved there during my stint in transit, started our first Chapter and has been moving out ever since. In the beginning, she set up shop in her home, turning one of her bedrooms into a small work place. After about a year of working out of her living quarters, eventually with the enormous support of so many well wishers, she was able to move into a spacious office on Main St. in downtown Richmond. Being a (non-profit org) we qualified to receive Government funding to assist in the Growth and Development of the organization. So between the Government Grants and generous donations pouring in from local businesses, as well as a host of prominent figures in the entertainment field, it gave us the thrust we needed to advance RISING SUN forward. This whole idea of unification amongst gangs and just regular street dudes was terrific and the timing for such an idea was ripe. The concept of RISING SUN, if adopted by the Black Community imparticular, but the whole society in general, meant a decrease in crime and senseless homicides.

We would inspire hope in a society filled with hopelessness. Black Pride and self love would be the basis on which educational institutions would be built for our ailing youth to be cultivated and prepared to compete with the best of society. Because the traditional educational process had been such a failure, we opted to create our own paradigm, our own system and take full responsibility of teaching our children properly. In my absence (prison) as Prina's hard work began to pay off and the organization started to get National attention, her schedule became a frenzy of engagements, radio interviews, and in-depth discussions with some of our most brilliant minds. Folks from all walks of life were interested in RISING SUN mainly because the whole idea was to uplift the community. Letters and emails would swarm in from young and older women, who were overly concerned about their adolescences, man child becoming a lost statistic. They wanted to get involved and there were some of them so determined about saving their babies that like Prina Carrington, they were willing to start Chapters in their perspective towns. All over the country, the cry was the same. Wherever there was massive, black on black killing and major gang influence, the residents there were in search for a solution. RISING SUN was about taking full responsibility for our actions and our neighborhoods and to stop looking for some imaginary force to come in and do for us what we could and should be doing for ourselves.

Heaven and Hell to me was simply two conditions of life. Our deteriorating neighborhoods were only a reflection of our sick and polluted minds. It's a no wonder our hoods was hot even in the chilly winter. It's a no wonder why garbage filled the streets and our young people resembled the living dead. Alive, yet not living so if we weren't living out our full potential, then in a sense, we were dead because to really live life, meant to be active. Let's just face it, a lot of us weren't doing squat. RISING SUN was simply saying that reality didn't have to be what it was. We could change it just by removing the debris from our minds and replacing it with more productive thoughts. Heaven could be here and now. We could transform our little drug infested Ghettos into a place of peace and paradise. To many this was simply a distant dream. Better said than done...I'm not talking about some exaggerated fancy of mine. No no...

This reconstruction I'm speaking of is happening, has happened in the city of Richmond Virginia where our main office is located. Not the work of RISING SUN however, but the "Prince Of Peace Foundation"...Just one of many corporations under the parent company, BLACK WALL STREET. Headed by Richmond's own giant, Percy "Prince" Miller, ex street hustler, self proclaimed self made millionaire extraordinaire, this cat had done more for the city in terms of community development and empowering young people to aspire to reach their highest potential, then any politician to date. Late 30's early 40's, give or take, ex convict said to have once sold everything on the city streets from cocaine, heroin, marijuana, hash, pills, even cough syrup. In an interview I read out of the Richmond Times, where Prince did a lecture before hundreds of college students at a Pep Rally held in the gymnasium of Virginia State, he claimed that the only thing he sells now days is growth and development and hope. He was definitely an inspiration to me. And I say this because, like so many successful people who obtain riches and leave the hood never looking back, he could've very easily taken the same route. But he didn't...He knew the significance the youth would play in the building of a new world. So instead of investing his wealth in frivolous things such as jewelry and fast cars...You know how we do, he set up institutions where youngsters could come and learn different trades. From plumbing, to electrician and AC maintenance, just to name few. Once they obtained the knowledge and completed the course through the (P.O.P) Foundation, he set up Mentoring Programs; also he provided legal assistance to troubled juveniles who were involved with the foundation.

Construction Companies, lucrative real estate investments, the list goes on but what mostly inspired me was that he was partly responsible for the transformation of two of the city's most crime stricken slums. I was beyond impressed. With our ideas being similar, it was only right that we merged. By the time of my release, RISING SUN had grown to a nationwide movement. Prina had done a magnificent job, making things so much easier for me upon release, financially and other wise. A red carpet was literally laid out for me and many important people were waiting to welcome me back to the world. And as a token of their appreciation for RISING SUN and the principles on which it stood, I was accommodated with lots of extravagant gifts. I'm talking top notch designer clothes, over a dozen custom made suits from some of the biggest names in fashion, not to mention a brand new fully equipped SUV with all the trimming. The vehicle was personally delivered to me, with the RISING SUN vanity plates and all by a very good friend in the music industry. While everyone expressed their gratitude and showered me with wonderful gifts, I in turn had to thank Allah for His mercy and His Grace. He promised me that if I submitted to do his will, that he'd send angels my way and provide me with friends from all walks of life...

Meanwhile, to add to all the excitement, my autobiography had been written by the most controversial, African American writer of the 21 century. But I had caught a lot of static and heated criticism because of my choice to allow my story to be told by The Ghost. He was a troublemaker and hate writer; anti this, anti that...Yeah right! In my eyes, he was a straight up realest, a warrior who didn't wither in the face of opposition, or hesitate to defend the defenseless. And besides all that, this brother was selling millions of books. This cat had a fan base out of this world, not just black folks but people of all hues were fascinated with his work. What confirmed it for me that this brother had made it big time, was when I was back in the penitentiary, searching for a novel to read on the book cart that officers rolled around every so often, I stumbled across one of the authors books printed in Spanish. It totally stunned me. I couldn't have chosen a better person to write my story, so to hell with what the hating critics were saying. In fact, upon my release, my autobiography was just about to go into print and was expected to do extremely well. The marketing team was superb. Not bad for an ex con, huh?

Richmond Virginia would become my new home. Naturally, it just made sense that I'd end up there, seeing as though, it's where our main base was. And of course, Prina was there...Our love for one another had deepened with time, so much so that the very idea of being some place other than near her seemed absurd. She had proved to me beyond a shadow of a doubt that she was down for me...down for the movement. To me, she was an amazing person, unlike any female specimen I'd ever encountered. Our relationship was a unique one, in the sense that we were able to build a strong friendship first. Long before any physical bonding, we had been stroking and stimulating each other mentally, which made all the difference. Our bond was built on something more than hot sweaty sex. Before all of that, we were in love. Upon my release, though Prina was in love with me and I was with her, would you believe that I was asked to take an HIV test before we could kill the enormous crave that had been intensifying between us for five long years. Such a request would offend most men but for me, for some strange reason, it was more to the contrary. Like anyone, my first reaction was shock. Most definitely, she caught a brother off guard but at no point did I feel offended. If anything, I respected her even more because of it. Too many of these women out here were easy access. They didn't respect themselves and allowed strange men into their beds and as a result, one morning they awakened suddenly with a death sentence. But Ms. Prina Carrington was a real woman in the true sense of the word. We both ended up testing and we both were well pleased with the results. After knowing one another's status, we didn't make love, we made Heaven together. It was something wonderful and indescribable. All I can say is, it was great to be back...

As a result of Prina's excellent networking skills, Richmond's Elite, like many admirers around the country, had an interest in our organization. I had been home about a month lounging and enjoying some quiet time around the house, when the call came in from Prince. We had spoken prior to this but it was very brief, more of a welcoming home address. On this particular day, he wanted me to accompany him and his entourage to a meeting at the East End Mosque where

Brother Minister, Kihiem Muhammad who I'd heard so much about was scheduled to speak. Of course, I accepted the invitation. With my Queen by my side and her son Doug Jr, we all piled up in the spacey SUV and headed across town to the engagement.

In attendance was five of the most influential and successful black families within the City of Richmond. The Crawford family owned one of the most successful neighborhood eateries and Soul food take outs for over fifty years. He owned eight restaurants in four different locations of the city. Edmond Jackson was the owner of his own Pharmacy in the Churchill area who serviced the community for over thirty years and held a seat on the city council for ten years. Al Brown owned several used car lots in the Southside of Richmond, very active in the community and owned the first black owned radio station in the city. Dr. James Royal, who for over 40 years practiced medicine, he was everyone's favorite doctor and a much respected figure in the city. And last was the Mayor, Lawrence Mundy who still held a prominent, strong hold on political issues in the community. Minister Kihiem Muhammad stood strong on the podium, adjusted his microphone at the perfect angle. He straightened his silk neck tie and then once again, he gave Allah all the praise and glory and began with his speech....

"Allah has provided us tonight brothers and sisters with a vision that hasn't been clear in the last eighty years in this country. We have not chosen this vision, this vision has chosen us. From Tulsa Oklahoma to Richmond VA, we are the vessels of the new Modern day *Black Wall Street*. Financial, economical and educational empowerment, ten years ago brothers and sisters, we represented 37% of the prison population. Thirty-seven percent and we only represented 12% of the country. Eighty-seven years ago over 3,000 of God's chosen originators were bombed from the air by devils driven by sheer hatred in Oklahoma's GAP neighborhoods. Those sacrificial lambs of Allah provided tonight's vision to be acknowledged as a very necessary movement, as well as a highly obtainable objective for us as a people. We are human missile interceptors. We who come humbly before Allah tonight, my family are the newly appointed originators of the New Millennium, **Black Wall Street**. With the guidance and assistance of Allah, we will fight tooth and nail for the future of our community's existence."

The temple exploded with applause and standing ovations as Kihiem gazed drifted out into the crowd, acknowledging the power of his words and the strength of his leadership. The community was coming together to share their vision. For years, Kihiem had been the messenger of hope to a community previously riddled with drugs, murder and poverty, and the appreciation was showed through applauses that lasted for two to three long minutes. As he went on to stress the importance of a unified force between the city's religious figures, he suddenly hesitated his next statement as a broad, authentic smile swept across his face. Taking a few seconds to scan his surroundings as the (Islam Nation) and GTs (Girls Training) members all positioned in their designated seats, some of them hugging the walls, due to the place being filled to its capacity. His eyes wandered until they spotted his partner and brother, Prince and the unfamiliar face seated on the first row.

"Family, we have a very special guest amongst us tonight. In the battle for our liberation as a people, we need all the strong warriors we can get. I thank Allah for our brother, Mr. Nat Turner and the idea He put in this brothers head to start an organization like RISING SUN...Brother would you please stand," Kihiem prompted the new comer as the audience exploded in applause. "We welcome you to our city and we here in the Islam Nation look forward to working with you in the near future. His gaze drifted back out into the audience again, he resumed. "There's a lot of potential here in Richmond. Progress is being made in our neighborhoods, one project at a time. Brothers and sisters, if we're serious about change, we can transform our down trodden Ghettos into a respective community. A community where little children can play safely without the fear of being caught in a led shower; where our elders could come out of their prisons and enjoy a nice peaceful moment on their porch. With the help of Allah we can do this. In time we can turn the city of Richmond into a model city for the country to reflect. Our President, Barrack Obama can't change the world all by himself. Let's show him and the world that we have the ability to do for selves. Everything we need people, God has already provided us with the necessary tools to work to prepare a future for our babies. We don't have to look no further than each other..."

Chapter

_6_

Kihiem's lecture produced quite a turnout. A very serious aura flooded through the temple as the Minister closed his address. And Nat...after leaving the meeting was simply invigorated with a passion to go straight to work. He was blown away by Brother Minister's enthusiasm for change and was eager to merge Black Wall St. and his own establishment, RISING SUN and take the city by storm. When the meeting was over, Nat was invited out to a restaurant owned by Prince. Star and Crescent's was one of the many legitimate establishments he'd successfully created in the hood between Creighton Brook and Fair Hill projects. The building was once a club owned by an old head gambler called Sonny. It sat on the corner of 29th and Nine Mile road. Creighton Brook and Fair Hill had once been a home to some of the most treacherous gangster's to walk the Richmond streets and Sonny's from Wednesday to Sundays was the night life spot that everyone patronized. The down side was that these two rival projects had a dark history of aggression toward one another. Shootings, robberies, drug deals and even rapes were regular occurrences for as long as Sonny's was in existence.

In years to come, Sonny's began its transformation from the Devils weapon to the tool of Allah's will. Star and Crescent specialized in health food, nutritious meals and tasty Muslim dishes prepared by the modest women in the Mosque. It had been redesigned and renovated beautifully with the Egyptian Architecture style and large Plasma Screens in the dining area. A 70' velvet painting of the Muslim leader, Minister FM set on the wall. Alongside Nat was Prince, Kihiem Muhammad, Reverend Rodney from the United Methodist church, not too far from the East end Mosque. They enjoyed good food while dialoging over different issues ranging from politics, race relations and most importantly, how they could come together for the betterment of the community. That following day, Nat was taken on an interesting tour through the city's roughest areas to view for himself, the remarkable works of the (P.O.P) Foundation in the Creighton Brook area, which was the very first project to be broken and rebuilt by the (P.O.P) Foundation. Nat marveled at the now peaceful and clean strip with project buildings lined snugly on either side. It was a beautiful spring day and a few older tenants sat on their porches enjoying the warmth with an occasional cool breeze, appreciating the pleasure of watching the small children play at the playground where it had once been a place of pure chaos. Once occupied by hood figures, crap shooters and constant drug sells but thanks to the reconstruction and working with the youth through the (P.O.P) Foundation, that nonsense was now a thing of the past.

With so many fathers missing in action, Mentorship Programs was a must. There were over a hundred Big Brother figures that disseminated all over the city wherever Black Wall St. put in work. The Big Brother's tutored the kids assigned to them and occasionally visited their perspective school's to participate in **Parent and Teacher's Conference.** Quality time was a requirement because too many ghetto children didn't have anyone to confide in. It was one hell of a system that Prince and his ace, Kihiem Muhammad had set up. Prince was a legend in the streets of Richmond and at just the mention of his name demanded respect and no one ever came short. After leaving the projects, the next order of business was in another dangerous hood. The Marcy neighborhood was located on the Southside of Richmond. The concrete, the bricks, the drugs, violence, poverty and hopeless figures was the next big challenge for Kihiem and the (P.O.P) Foundation. It would probably be the most difficult shell to crack because Marcy Projects had always been regulated by major players with iron fist. Drugs, money and more murder were the top three commandments and had been for some time. It was similar to how the children in Iraq were born and bred for the sake of Jihad. Except in Marcy, children were born and bred to uphold those three commandments that their neighborhood was built upon, drugs, money and murder. Every young child had a right to grow up in a drug free environment. Until the coming of Black Wall St, this city had never seen anything like what was taking place. The whole operation was originally the brain child of Kihiem Muhammad, who brought the idea to his long time friend Prince. Already a real estate giant and a significant factor in the Richmond community from his affiliation with the Boys and Girls Club Chapters and numerous other ventures, Prince didn't hesitate to aid his partner. With millions on top of millions of dead presidents sitting away in some bank collecting interest, while his most precious jewels were withering away in some prison cell, or dying out right in the unforgiving streets, Prince thought, 'Why not use my fortune to improve life here in the city.'

While the Government set out to push residents out of the city and knock down their homes under the guise of gentrification, Prince was making arrangements to purchase a whole damn project. The city was changing rapidly with the Governments so called reconstruction. Residents who had lived in the Cap City their entire lives were now being ushered out and scattered about like refugees. So much struggle and tremendous life lost within these streets, young black lives slaughtered effortlessly without conscious or real cause. And now…they were raising the rent and as a result, residents caught a raw deal. Kihiem Muhammad saw through the Government's deceitful façade. In the past life, he sold death in his own neighborhood; he'd been a murderer of his own kind, went into federal prison to serve nearly twenty straight years, and now he was back on the same decadent streets he'd once terrorized, attempting to clean up the mess. The same enthusiasm he took to the streets as a drug dealer, he did the same as a truth fighter. He explained the aim of the Government to anyone who would listen.

Meanwhile, behind the scenes, Black Wall St. was being brought into fruition. Documents were produced and signed, mergers were started and large prepositions were discussed to get the ball rolling. The idea was to sort out urban blighted neighborhoods, purchase the property and disrupt the gentrification process. Prince's idea to enrich and help the lives of tenants who would otherwise have no hope in the city wouldn't set well with city officials once they got wind of it. This he was sure of. But the ball had already begun to roll and Prince's resources and support system was solid. Money talked and bullshit walked a thousand miles. All the information he needed was provided by a powerful research team, his loyal attorneys moved with thorough efficiency and by his side like a black berry, was his mentor and attorney, the Brother Shabazz. These two men were inseparable, Prince hardly ever traveled anywhere without him. With a legal counsel always around to advise, it left little room for foolish mistakes.

Jacky Williams, representative of the alliance to conserve old Richmond Neighborhoods shared Black Wall St. vision in their desire to preserve the perishing inner city. There was a lot of red tape and mind blowing opposition in the beginning to prevent the mission, but in the end, Black Wall St. prevailed. Kihiem Muhammad and the Islam Nation had put in some serious ground work in the city. They knocked on doors, had flyers printed out to promote the unification and cleaning up of the neighborhoods and summoned for tenants to support it. They put together functions, held town hall meetings for everyone to come out and voice their own opinions. This type of mobilization went on for months, nearly six long months and when it was over, Black Wall St. had won the hearts of the people. Contrary to what some may believe, the Richmond residents, for the most part were appalled at how indecent their neighborhoods had become. Change was a must. "The number one rule when building something solid," Prince would often say to the Forman of his construction co. before undergoing a project. "It's imperative to begin with a firm foundation. Put down the floor first, then the walls go up and after the walls, the ceiling, etc."

He'd continue, "Only a tree with weak roots crumbles under a storm. There's no need to build where there's still destruction in process." So with that said, Black Wall St, the (P.O.P) Foundation's first objective was to rid the projects of destruction by any means. In no way was this task easy, in fact, it was a struggle between good and evil. It took a while to get through to the hustlers because the neighborhood was where they conducted business, did their dirt all at the expense of their own people and community. With the residents soldering behind and determined to see change, the opposing youngsters eventually folded? In a year's time, Fair Hill projects were totally free of crime. From Phillip's to Rosetta st, the only thing you could find to buy was icebergs, candy and occasionally a mixed drink from one of the many bootleg establishments, which was respectfully approved by Prince. A lot of the street dealers either joined the movement or fled to someplace else to distribute their poison. Once the garbage was out, the (P.O.P) Foundation moved in. Of course, there were problems on top of problems. Drug addiction and illiteracy was at the top of the list. The American education system wasn't a challenge for the youth of today and as a result, they developed a distaste for learning. The youth being the number one priority, the mentorship program was quickly established. Every problem had a solution.

As it had always been in the past, so many doubted....hated on the idea of two ex street felon's being responsible for such a wonderful idea. No one could reach these lost souls is what a lot of folks claimed. But they got the shock of a life time. The project proved to be a success. Community development was the basis of self improvement. Kihiem Muhammad's aim was to first build human potential, set institutions of learning where residents could come and be taught history and the true knowledge of themselves. The

Brother Minister wasn't interested in trying to convert people to Islam. What he wanted was to build awareness and lift the brothers and sisters self esteem so that they could start to see themselves and one another in a new light. The community saw the effort these brothers were putting forth on their behalf and so after months and months of resistance, the entire neighborhood suddenly came together to make a nonbinding oath. They had come to the realization that what the organization was offering, was best for everyone involved, not to mention the youth. This was an opportunity, finally to put an end to the vicious cycle of ignorance, where innocent little ones would have a chance at greatness, instead of being systematically duped into a life of crime. Directly across the street from the hood where Fair Hill swimming pool once resided, the plain was remedied and transformed into the very first Youth Center of its kind. Those who were opposed to the ideas of Black Wall St. and there were many, didn't see the significance in investing the time and money in such a ravaged neighborhood. Prince was mocked and called a damned fool by his peers and some of the boot licking politicians in the city for spending well over a quarter of a million of his own hard earned dollars to build the center. Recognition for their contributions hardly ever received any publicity and when they did, the papers never failed to down play their efforts. Never-the-less, none of that stopped what was meant to be.

In a year's time, the Youth Center was finished and a new spirit of togetherness began to manifest in the Fair Hill residents. Through the weekly informative town hall meetings, they were gradually learning that their lives had purpose. And also, scholarships were offered to ten percent of the eligible residents of Fair Hill if, in fact, they met the specific criteria based solely on their participation in the approved curriculum. This alone gave students drive and ambition to improve their grades. The biggest obstacle in trying to implement this new program to the people was not the young brothers in the streets, but surprisingly the boys in blue. One would think that the Police Department would appreciate and embrace such a program that brought calm over a once disruptive community but sadly, that was not the case. Pathetically, it was foul and downright evil police officers who terrorized and unsuccessfully tried to compromise (P.O.P's) efforts in the neighborhood. The absurd idea of redevelopment and ridding the place of crime meant less arrest for the uniforms. They made it more than clear, that their aim was not to fight crime but the contrary. It frustrated the hell out of these cops to ride through their designated territories and not have a reason to jump out. But of course, that didn't stop them...

They began a series of harsh intimidation tactics on the area residents, stop in search, verbally abusing them and just acting a straight up fool. When that weak tactic failed, they took it a step further. Drugs that the corrupt bastards probably confiscated off of some poor street hustler, they'd turn right back around and give it to one of their snitches willing to cut their brothers throat to save their own asses. The informer was instructed to go into the drug free neighborhood with a sack filled with narcotics and post up, where that same officer who gave him the drugs would come back and arrest him on possession charges. The media would jump all over this and put the organization on blast. Prince had a lengthy history with the Richmond law enforcement. One can never truly separate their past from the present, however if they're crafty enough, they can manipulate the present to make people forget the past as their eyes looks toward the future. Somehow, he doubted that he'd ever be accepted by the Police Department and their bullshit politics. He had defied the odds, slipped through the cracks of incarceration and went on to become a success story.

"It ain't how far you fall down, but how high you bounce back." Those words said to Prince almost twenty years ago by his mentor still echoed into his conscious even until this day. In whatever endeavor he found himself engaged in, he kept those principles dear and never faltered, always reaching for the stars. Money had once been his sole motivation, but now with this new project, the revitalization of the torn neighborhoods and insisting in the cultivation of young people to help them achieve their goals, his life had suddenly taken on new purpose. Community activism had always been a passion of his but now it had become the center of his existence. Within a year's time of (P.O.P) Foundation's intervention in the Fair Hill Housing Projects, one could take a stroll through the once shabby streets and see the dramatic change. The days of seeing littered filled streets, loitering, public drunkenness and crime in the neighborhood was long gone. After a while even the hustlers who had once occupied every crack and cranny of the hood, started to show appreciation for the work of the (P.O.P) Foundation.

What type of man would slang poison to his own kind, in his own neighborhood, where the family and the children had to grow up? Kihiem Muhammad and the (P.O.P) Foundation in the infancy stages would hold forums out in the community and invite just the hustlers to come and share dialogue. It proved to be the most effective alternative way to reach them. Though they were a different breed of young men than from Prince and Kihiem's era, they all seemed to have heard about the legendary Juice Crew. That fact alone was the main reason that the new generation was more subject to listen. It was just an inspiration in itself to see someone like themselves doing something as profound like trying to clean up the neighborhoods. Kihiem Muhammad would have heart-to-heart conversations with these brothers about how drugs were purposely distributed throughout the once stable communities to create havoc and cause imbalance, ultimately turning a people inside out. In a time where "so called" men of God got little or no respect from the street dwellers, particularly due to a lot of them continuously bullshitting the people and tickling their ears with empty speeches; Kihiem Muhammad was able to calm them. They knew without doubt or contradiction that the (P.O.P) Foundation, the Islam Nation was for them.

Black Wall St. was not simply involved in the revitalization of neighborhoods but the core essence of what this movement was about, besides improving black life, was creating economic empowerment. Reestablishing black owned businesses in the community where everyone, but the inhabitant's seemed to prosper. Black folks were the biggest consumers of America's goods, but didn't produce squat. What a shame. Black Wall St. had set up a chain of grocery stores, laundry mats and restaurants around the city, mainly in areas where the organization sort interest. The whole idea was to encourage folks to support their own, especially an organization who willingly gave back to the community. The residents responded and before long, other neighborhoods wanted to adopt the concept...For the (P.O.P) Foundation to come into their tarnished neighborhoods, clean out the garbage and restore some order, Marcy residents made an impression. They had heard about the remarkable work from friends and family members who'd committed themselves to helping the (P.O.P) Foundation clean up their neighborhoods. Recognition for the (P.O.P) movement stayed at a minimum until the coming of the talented journalist, Ms. Prina Carrington. A true freedom fighter, as well as a growing celebrity for her well informed columns covering a range of important issues involving the community. But most importantly, her most recent articles written on the new establishment, RISING SUN, is what earned her the attention of giants like Prince and a host of other important people in the City. She was taken aback upon arriving into Richmond and witnessing with her own two eyes, the works of the (P.O.P) Foundation. These now re-formed neighborhoods were nothing like she'd remembered as a young teeny bopper, tearing through the city streets. So impressed by Black Wall St. community development pro-grams and numerous other business ventures, she didn't waste time in contacting the establishment. And before anyone could blink, she had begun writing articles on Black Wall St's influence on the Richmond community. Her sudden transfer from the Washington Post to the Richmond Times Dispatch was undoubtly a blessing to the city.

Meanwhile RISING SUN was embraced and the Black Wall St. establishment assisted the journalist in starting the very first RISING SUN Chapter in the city, providing her with an office building and the whole nine. So by the time of Nat Turner's release, the set up that awaited him on the outside was nothing short of phenomenal. Honey had worked her butt off and put everything on the line to see the organization as

Nat had envisioned it. She pooled every possible resource and in her travels, she made healthy connections with some of the most influential names in the country. She met folks who not only respected and shared the desire to see an end to the gang violence, but also willing to contribute to the cause.

Like mother Coretta Scott, Prina embodied that same courageous spirit to not only hold down the fort in her man's absence but she knew what she wanted and exactly how to get it. (She was a go getter.) Because of her hard work and constantly being on top of Nat affairs while he was away, his long awaited autobiography was about to hit the shelves with a vengeance. The book was so highly anticipated, that the company publishing the project had over 500,000 books in print ready to be distributed to every major retail store across the country. Nat's release couldn't have come at a better time. There were handsome build boards in place promoting the books release in numerous parts of the country, radio personnel dialoguing about it on their respective stations. The publicity surrounding this brother's life story was unreal. From the news reporters, to famous talk show host who wanted to have him on for an interview, everyone seemed to want a piece of him. Speaking engagements were also at his disposal. As soon as he was ready, there was a long list of folks who were actually willing to pay a fee, in exchange for Nat to come and speak. Upon learning of his release, everyone from high school principles to even college professors, shot invitations at him. And none of this would be possible if in fact, Prina Carrington hadn't come along when she did.

In helping Nat establish RISING SUN, she in return helped herself as well. Her only desire was to save her son from becoming a statistic. The organization had not only saved

Doug Jr. but it was gradually making a man of him. These days, he was just as committed to the movement as her, which was heartwarming to witness. Not only did it make her extra proud, but it was also a huge relief to see Doug Jr. and Nat inner acting so closely. She could sense a tight bond brewing. In this day and most troublesome time, a positive role model in the "Hood" was like searching for a needle in a haystack. But Nat had made such an impression on her son. Before Nat, none of her guy friends over the years could ever get close to him. Nat however was a different story. It was obvious why she was so caught up on this brother. There was nothing more attractive to a real woman then the sight of a strong and ambitious man who knew his destiny. She was so turned on by that quality in Nat. And though she approved of the arrangements with the two men in her life, she couldn't help but wonder about their connection. Doug Jr. was really drawn to him. Other than the fact that Nat's vision had given both their lives new meaning, Prina often times felt that there was more that meets the eye. Like maybe he'd found something very magnificent that had been gravely, snatched away from him long ago. In many ways, Nat was a lot like Doug, her deceased husband so thought Prina. Both men were unique in their own way. She could recall how Doug would express with passion his desire to see the neighborhoods crime free. He wanted his two children to receive a full and complete education, grow up well informed and utilize their skills to be contributors to society. This was Doug's dream before his death; too bad things didn't turn out as he'd hopped.

Chapter

7

Nat Turner

My homecoming was truly something monumental. I didn't expect to be accepted by so many wonderful people. Prina, my queen had represented me well. Because of the foundation she's laid, every neighborhood we visited, the folks out there knew something of RISING SUN. In Richmond, gangs weren't as prevalent as they were all across the country, however the street violence was just as horrific as it was anywhere else. Though the (P.O.P) Foundation was already doing a spectacular job in the city, still I felt like Richmond was the perfect place to setup shop. We all wanted the same thing. These brothers were already doing what I was attempting to try and do. But what wasn't in place and desperately needed, was an organization that specifically targeted gangs, young men imparticular. I wasn't concerned with being the leader of nothing. I simply wanted to get in where I fitted in. A winning team is where I desired to be. The Black Wall St. establishment was definitely on point. RISING SUN was no light weight organization, which was why so many embraced us. In some of our discussions, Kihiem would always say to me before we parted ways, that Allah held me in high favor. 'Keep Him at the Head, brother and your success is imminent.'

Within two months of my release, I had calls coming in from as far as Chicago, California and Saint Louis, states where gang banging was the most notorious. The community leader and gangbangers out there wanted to start their own branches. This thing was spreading so fast that I was up around the clock, working like a mad man trying to build RISING SUN into an empire. So I began accepting invitations to speak about the organizations aim at different high schools and colleges local and abroad. On a mission to recruit new members, we did the same thing in the neighborhoods. Following (P.O.P) Foundation's lead, we'd urge residents to take charge of their community and help us build something that our children could be proud of.

I had a lot of ideas to add. I had my eyes set on some foreclosure property located in North side off of Nine mile road. Once upon a time, the building had been a popular Super Market but I had plans to turn it into a gymnasium where we would conduct everything from self defense classes to even training youngsters how to box. Our youth had too much idle time on their hands, so in setting up institutions where they could come and be educated on a range of important issues, while also having the option to do some athletic training, that alone would minimize the chances of them committing petty crimes! At least it was a start. I wanted to make RISING SUN just as attractive to the young mind, as the Bloods/Crips was or any other gang that drew our adolescence in like magnets. The only difference would be that, we'd be building up ourselves and our neighborhoods instead of destroying them. It took me nearly six months to get fully established after being away for so long. But once I was back, I was back.

My story was expected to be a big success, the company even predicted to sell a million copies by the year's end. Could you believe that? A million people interested in Nathanial Turner. The more traveling and networking I did, the more the memberships began to grow. I made trips across the continent, Chi Town, LA, Saint Louis and just about every place that I went, branches were eventually setup. In these major cities, gangbangers from all walks of life came out to listen to what we had to say. I'm talking Hispanic and Mexicans brothers who'd heard about the organization, had purchase and read my autobiography, attended the events as well. As I stood before the diverse crowds, I was reminded of my time in prison when I spoke to hundreds of prisoners about the need for an organization like mine. And less than 24 hours later, I barely escaped a vicious death plot. In order for me to seriously affect my people, I knew that I couldn't be fearful of them. So I took my show on the road, crashing some of the most dangerous areas in the country, knowing that many of the hoods I visited were filled with brothers who packed more heat than a Bill Cosby sweater. On my journey, I rubbed shoulders with legends like Jim Brown, a real warrior of the streets. I was truly a fan. For years on top of years, he'd been working strenuously with gangbangers through his anti gang organizations. All across the board, I received praise for my efforts in trying to launch such a movement as trying to bring the gangs together. I wasn't at all naïve and never once did I ever expect it to be a walk in the park. But I had a vision; I was called on to do this work.

No one organization could go at our problems alone, which is why no matter where my successes lead me, at the end of day, my heart's desire was to be in the city of Richmond, helping the (P.O.P) establishment finalize what they started. And that was, to rebuild the ailing neighborhoods and its people through the awesome system they put together. I wanted to be a part of that. In fact, I made a courageous move. In the middle of a breakfast meeting with Prince and Kihiem, I asked if I could assist them in the next big project. The cleaning up of Marcy Projects was no light weight thing. Truthfully, it was (P.O.P's) biggest challenge yet. The neighborhood housed some vicious street cats who weren't necessarily in agreement with the cleaning process. But the residents were fed up and wanted change. It was them who wanted the (P.O.P) Foundation to come in and set up shop. Elders like Ms. Betty Lee who'd spent over four decades out there and had watched the neighborhood slowly and painfully deteriorate in that time. If there was anything you needed to know about that area, she was the person to talk to. From Kihiem, I learned on our way over to meet with her, that she'd lost three sons who were all murdered years ago on these very same streets not too far from where she currently lived. These projects left Ms Betty Lee with only one child alive. Her daughter Tee Tee was at the present serving a 15 sentence in Fluvanna women's facility.

These days, Ms. Betty Lee sits on her front porch a lot and sells candy, cigarettes and mixed drinks or beer from the back door. She is never lonely because she's the mother of Marcy Projects. She lost her own children to the streets but in return, the streets provided her with many more. The ones that were neglected by cracked out mothers, Ms. Lee took them in. Even the ones in trouble with the law would sometimes take shelter at Ms Betty Lee's home. She was a big woman in statue, as well as reputation in the projects. Respected by all the worse killers and dope fiends that these gutters had ever produced, no one could ever forget how her boys put these projects on the map. When they were alive, it was said that Marcy Projects was similar to Harlem. Nothing but the flyest cars in the city lined these streets. All the hustlers from all over had to come through there and get accommodated at that time. The sack chasers flocked to these streets when Chaz, Brock and Red had it on lock. But those were the days; Ms. Betty Lee now carries the torch for hers.

When we arrived at Ms. Betty Lees, it was still kind of early, but the morning heroin game was in full affect. The addicts were stumbling past, trying to find a safe place to get medicated after quickly scoring their first shot of the day. It was real out here and from just minutes of observing the pitiful display, I knew right off that we had our work cut out for us. Ms. Betty Lee, I admired her at first glance. Just a couple minutes in her company, you got the feeling that you'd known her for some time. She did most of the talking while Kihiem and I listened, my eyes never leaving the early morning action in the street a few feet away. Obviously, Kihiem and Ms. Betty Lee had a history because she never once called him by his Muslim name but by Justice, his old street name. Until now, I had never heard anyone address him as that.

"Just", Ms Betty Lee started. "I sho do miss my boys...They just took them away from me just like that. One by one, first Red and then Brock the same night and my youngest one, Chaz less than 6 months later, now tell me I ain't strong to not have went crazy after all that." The old woman let out a cackle." You know I'm 68 years old now."

"Is that right," Kihiem said. "You could've fooled me; I could've sworn you were just 25."

"Yeah me too," I added and laughter was shared between the three of us. It was nice to see Ms. Betty Lee smile. I wondered did she get to do it often. But just as quick as the smile came, it vanished.

"Forty years I've been living in this neighborhood and I've never seen shit as bad as it is now." Shaking her head in disgust at a couple addicts taking cover at the playground across the street where the neighborhood children once played, she continued, "Don't look like its gonna get better, either."

"See, ma that's the whole thing in a nut shell right there", Kihiem began. "The only way it's gonna better out here, is if we put forth the effort and make it better ourselves. Not the Mayor, nor the police force, but us. We've been sitting ducks for much too long now, waiting for others to do for us, what we could and should be doing for ourselves."

"I love it when he talks like that. If it takes going to prison for a man to turn out like you did, Justice then a lot of these little bad ass wanna be gangsters need to go to jail. I hate to put it like that, but it's true."

"Ms. Betty Lee, prison was never meant to rehabilitate us." I cut in. "In fact, it's only a warehouse and don't but a few make it out like Brother Kihiem here. To the institutions delight, a lot of brothers just wither away from a broken spirit and a lack of hope in the system and most importantly, themselves. Don't get me wrong now because prison can be a wonderful experience for those of us who can humble ourselves enough to hear the voice of God."

"Amen," Ms. Betty Lee raved. "Feel like I'm in church out here. Go head boy!"

"There ain't' no bling, bling, or thousand stacks to count up, all the material things that clouds our vision while out in the streets is stripped away when we enter these institutions. And so God has access to us now. It's easy for a brother to find religion in prison. But in order for change to really happen in you, you gotta want it bad."

"Well there's one thang for sho', this boy here..." She gestured at Kihiem seated across from her. "The only way I'd recognize him is by that handsome face of his cause he ain't nothing like I remember. He's so respectful and humble now. I mean this boy was bad ass hell." Ms. Betty Lee cuts an eye over at Kihiem, "he done went and turnt Mooslem now. Who would've ever thought?" Ms. Betty let out a cackle at her own joke and so did I and Kihiem. She laughed out loud while rocking back and forth in her chair, as if she hadn't laughed in years. It was such a joy to see that, given all the strife she'd endured over the years with the lost of her children.

"Do ya'll really think there's hope for this neighborhood? It's so bad out here and these youngsters out here don't care about nothing."

"There's always hope ma," Kihiem said. "You see what we've done with the other neighborhoods, don't you. They were all bad at one time but now for the most part, they're clean. It'll surprise you to find out that a lot of youngsters you see out here probably hate what they're doing. A lot of us hustle because of the lack of resources and proper guidance."

"It won't be easy," I told Ms. Betty Lee

"Lord knows we need some help out here. And my grand kids, they out in these streets trying to follow right in their father's footsteps, they don't listen to a word I say. I tell 'em all the time that everything they out here doing, somebody else done already did. I done seen the end result to this shit. And I just pray that the good Lord above take me away from here first, before I have to bury another one of my babies." Ms. Betty Lee sighed and shook her head. "Jesus Christ, my poor heart just can't take no more."

It's a damned shame when the parent out lives the child. It wasn't supposed to be that way, yet everything now a day seemed to be all screwed up. That day we sat and let the old lady babble on and on about her hopes and fears. And one couldn't help but feel compassion after listening to Ms. Betty Lee. I also notice as she was talking an expression on brother Kihiem's face that I had never seen before. An undeniable sadness that reassured me of the passion he embodied for his work. He really cared about the people he was trying to help. Ms. Betty Lee helped us organize the Marcy residents and two weeks later, we all packed up together for a town hall meeting at the neighborhood Rac Center. During this engagement, residents got a chance to air out their concerns and man; they sat that place on fire. Not literally, but the topics were hot.

"The police-officers are worse than the drug dealers," said one angry mother who'd lost both her sons by the hands of brutal cops. One killed by a stray police bullet and her baby boy, she said was a first time offender serving a twenty year sentence in federal prison. A grieving father there had some words to say. Six months earlier, his sixteen year old daughter was the victim of a hateful slug that smashed into her skull, while sitting by her bedroom window doing her homework. Poor girl didn't stand a chance; she died on the spot, the result of a moronic drive by shooting. A lot of pain and simmering frustration filled that room, but when it was all said and done, one thing was clear. Every resident present that day and there was many; they all had one thing in common. And that was an ultimate desire for change.

On that day, we all made a commitment. Against all odds, we would all strive to improve the neighborhood and recruit as many young people as we could. After all, it was all about the youth anyway. Millions of dollars had been dished out by the newly elected mayor to rebuild certain areas in the city. Deteriorating parks and unused abandon buildings had received reconstruction. Downtown also underwent a makeover. I was all for improving the city's infrastructures so that it'll look appealing to the eye; however why wasn't a potion of the tax payer's dollars being allocated to improve the flawed education system. To me, it seems as though their only solution for tackling the problems in the inner city, was to strengthen their police force. The penal system was their solution for the young and restless. So RISING SUN and the (P.O.P) Foundation were stepping up and doing our part. And we weren't against working with law enforcement to establish peace within the community. It was the other way around, the (P.O.P) Foundation and *Black Wall st.* was an embarrassment to the entire police force.

The so called **'War On Drugs'** had left the streets naked with the exception of the new up and coming dealers. And despite the magnitude of countless arrests, law enforcement was no closer to ridding the streets of drugs. What the (P.O.P) Foundation had done with the neighborhoods was absolutely incredible and the cops, who'd once patrolled the streets, stalking dealers like animal prey, hated it because it meant for them less arrest. On top of that, they were especially displeased with the idea of the I.N. having any involvement in the transformation taking place in the city. In a month's time

after a few more town halls and in-depth discussions with the
opposition (drug dealers), we slowly began to move in to the
Marcy neighborhood.

In the beginning, we caught hell from those who valued
the dollar bill over a drug free neighborhood. To have a drug
free neighborhood meant interfering with their cash flow and
it takes more than a good speech to try and change their
minds. The economy was shot to hell, jobs were scarce and the
price of living had sky rocketed over the years. Between those
factors and child support, sucking the blood out of a brother,
many didn't have much of a choice but to slang the devil's
poison. So telling these guys to drop and stop what they were
doing, was like speaking some type of foreign language. But of
course, I had to learn that the hard way. After a couple of close
encounters in which I almost got my head blown off, I change
my approach real quick.

It was mid July, hot and sunny out and we'd been working
in the neighborhood just a little over two months. Missy,
Donna and Damon, my little helpers were tagging along with
me while I tossed dirty syringes, crack viles and all kinds of
drug paraphernalia in a plastic trash bag. We were trying to
reclaim the children's playground. My back was facing the
street and I didn't see the Black Impala drive up or the
youngster who couldn't have been know more than 18 years
old exit the car. By the time Missy had gotten my attention, the
guy had closed in on me, weapon drawn and aimed at my
dome, right between my eyes.

I waved the children off, told them to get the hell away
from here. Looking at this kid, I was old enough to be his
father. In his eyes, I saw nothing there. I could tell that he was
a straight up gun slinger, young treacherous killer and taking

my life would mean nothing to him. He ordered me down to my knees and although shaken, I didn't budge. I stood motionless, totally clueless as to what had brought this about.

I said, "in front of these kids, you would do this. And for what reason do you want to take my life…No if this is my time to die then I gotta die standing, not on my knees." My heart quaked with fear, I can't lie. I flinched, waiting for the blast, staring through the barrels death tunnel but nothing ever happened. We held each other's gaze for eternity it seemed and then all of a sudden, his eyes left mine. I followed them, shifting my head slightly only to find an enraged 68 year old lady swearing and pointing from her porch across the street. She called the boy by his name (Corey) then told him to get lost because she'd already given the "Boys in Blue" a call. Inching backwards, Corey lowered the pistol and in a matter of seconds the little bastard had jump back onto the Impala. Tears burned my eyes watching the car speed away.

The beast inside me came alive and in that brief instant, my mind began to give birth to all sorts of murderous thoughts. I would be lying through my teeth to say that I didn't want to hurt that brother at that particular moment. First and foremost, I'm a street cat raised and bred from the rough, so naturally that violent street mentality kicked in. And though I was no longer a pistol totter, as I stood there fuming, my adrenaline on full blast, I wanted one badly. It was that old beast in me. We constantly battled each other, but somehow, I always managed to prevail. What bothered me mostly about the youngster was not necessarily the act in itself but the fact that he would snuff me out at the blink of an eye for absolutely nothing. But at first mention of the cops coming, he takes off. But just a minute ago, he was a gangster. I thank Allah for brothers like Kihiem because that incident almost sent me over the edge and it was my beloved brother who brought me all the way back to my senses.

Not even 20 minutes had passed after the encounter, when I spotted his big boy Black on Black F-150 pickup truck; bending the corner along with three *Black Wall St.* SUV's in tow. He'd obviously been contacted and informed about my run in. I later found out that Ms. Betty Lee caught the action from her living room window, got straight on the telephone and dialed the number to *Black Wall st.* headquarters. So she hadn't called the police after all, but it was a nice bluff, one that possibly saved my life. I learned from that episode, the clout that old lady had in her neighborhood. She was no one to take lightly or underestimate because of her old age. Ms. Betty Lee hadn't lived 68 years for nothing. She knew the streets better than most hustlers. I followed Kihiem across town where we stopped at Star and Crescent for some delicious bean soup and some conversation. On Kihiem heels, we entered the restaurant and were immediately greeted by a lovely smile and warm hospitality. Sister Fatimah, a member of Islam Nation and part time employee, escorted us to Kihiem's usual table in the rear of the restaurant facing the front entrance. I suppose he sat there to get a clear view of the oncoming traffic. But today, the atmosphere was serene as it had always been whenever I visited. Jill Scott's sweet soulful vocals filled the room as we sat. By this time, I wasn't as rattled up as I had been an hour earlier. And for what had happened, I only had myself to blame. Kihiem and the brothers had warned me about being out in the Marcy Projects alone, particularly because I was still a new face out there. No one really knew who I was other than the residents. It was still too early and we hadn't even scratched the surface of doing what we set out to do. A lot of hustlers felt as though we were trying to bully them off of their block. And in a sense, I guess they were right.

"Before you even say it," I started, anticipating Kihiem's remark before he could even open his mouth. "You were right, I was wrong, brother." Kihiem released a smile.

"Brother what the hell did you think you were doing? You know I wasn't gonna let you off the hook,"

"Obviously, I wasn't thinking brother." I shook my head and sighed like a troubled child being scorned by his big brother. I really admired Kihiem and I respected and valued his opinion so when he chastised me, I didn't open my mouth because I was taught that listening was more important than talking.

"It's a blessing brother that you're sitting here right now. It's more than evident that Allah is with you. But you must listen brother, Nat because there ain't a lot of room for slip-ups. These youngsters out here will body you quicker than you can blink. So why are you sitting here brother and not laying in the streets dead? It's because you are a part of God's plan. The idea inside your head man is so brilliant. Already, your organization has reached nationwide status. Your autobiography is already a best seller! Everybody who's somebody knows about RISING SUN. Do you think that's your work, brother...?"

"It's Allah work, brother."

"And don't you ever forget it, Nat...because the moment you do, the moment you take Allah out of the equation and exalt yourself as god beside God, brother that will be the beginning of your end. Tell me Nat; how you felt about the brother who pulled the pistol on you...I'm curious."

I knew where this conversation was leading to. What the hell type question was that anyway. How would any sane person feel about a person pointing a gun at their noggin? I mean come on."

"Brother I'm only human."

"Then keep it one hundred. It's just us talking here. We brother's right"

"Right, we are." I agreed.

"So...tell me. How did you fee-"

"I wanted to slump that little fucker, okay. "I leaned forward and whispered this." Excuse my language man."

"It's alright, I understand..."

"But those were my thoughts honestly, brother Kihiem. I wanted to take it back to the streets for a minute."

"I can relate, brother trust me. I've had my moments of doubt and insecurity. Not unsure about the truth that we represent but about our duty and the sacrifices that must be made in order to be effective in raising our people up. But men run to responsibility, boys run from it. This burden we must bear."

"Yeah, you right."

"Sister Harriet Tubman said it best. She said she could've freed more slaves if only they knew they were slaves. And that's us right now. Our people are sick brother Nat, but they think they are well. Now the brother you had the altercation with is sick but he doesn't know it. As difficult and as crazy as this may sound, Nat we truly have to love our people more than they hate themselves. As believers it says in the Koran that we'll be tested on that which we claim to believe. You were tested today brother, and you'll be tested again and again...But it's how you react to that test that determines the outcome, as well as your growth and development. With the proper guidance, that same young brother who violated you can be a warrior for Allah. So brother we gotta rise above our emotions and into the thinking if God. Your autobiography is one of the best books I've read in a long time. And what moved me the most about it was your ability to unite and bring brothers together. But then your brush with death is what really made the suns rise, (Brothers coming together.) Actually, you were being used as an instrument, I liked how that unfolded. Nat, how do you think *Black Wall St.* has had the success it's had?"

"Indulge me."

"We know our brothers out here. It would be foolish of us to go out into to these Projects and ask these guys to stop slanging the poison in the neighborhood. This is their lively hood, this is how they feed and clothe their families. You don't get something for nothing out here. This ain't prison, its real out here and brothers got responsibilities. We first educate them on how wicked and unjust the judicial system is, give them incarceration statistics and show them why they should give up the devil's way of life. We don't just tell them to stop slanging without having something to offer them in return. So *Black Wall St.* set up businesses and we give our people jobs so that they could continue to provide for their family. It may not be the type of cash they're used to, but it's enough to keep their head above water, plus they get to duck the penitentiary. And instead of being a part of the problem, they're now working to rebuild their tarnished neighborhoods into respective communities. It's a sweet deal for everyone involved..."

For some strange reason, when we got together, we auto-matically clicked. Only a fool could deny the truth that he spoke and so I would just sit and soak everything in. That discussion lasted well over two hours and as we parted for the night, I walked away inspired. While my focus was to build a nationwide movement, *Black Wall St.* was set on transforming the city of Richmond into a model for the country. I didn't realize until after leaving the meeting with Kihiem, the extent of their enterprise.

I knew nothing of the forty acres of land located just outside of the city limits in Chester, where the *Black Wall St.* establishment had reserved with plans to build a University. In addition to that, the *BLACK WALL ST.* dream team had a chain of black owned beauty supply stores. This was by far no easy accomplishment, given the foreigners disposition of conducting business with anyone other than their own people. But a new day was dawning in the Richmond community, thanks to *Black Wall St.* Block by block, they were taking over, not by flooding the hoods with bricks of China White but they were changing the status quo and creating their own reality by spreading the seed of life and economic empowerment. In my opinion, Prince and brother Kihiem were living legends in the flesh for real. They were doing what every true black man in the position to help the less fortunate should do. And often times, just being in their presence and witnessing the effect of their work, I'd get to feeling as though I was out of my league. But every man had their place...their part to play in the struggle...

Chapter

8

Businesses As Usual

P rince leaned back in the swivel chair made from genuine leather and commenced staring over the city of Richmond, admiring the smooth flow of the evening traffic. Absorbed by the peaceful quietness of his own thoughts, Prince had indeed come a long way from the streets of Richmond to his own plush office with a wonderful view in one of the many historical structures of downtown Richmond. Top floor of the James Center, today was a very busy day for Prince and his friend, mentor and attorney, the Brother Shabazz. Today was also a very big day for the Growth for his Parent business, *Black Wall Street.* The right moves and right connections equaled power. So much had been accomplished. It seemed that the city of Richmond and state of Virginia as a whole had in fact underestimated the potential growth of the ideas of the ex street hustler. Today's meeting had skyrocketed Prince from local to international. And to his future adversaries, he would prove to be a more than capable contender in achieving his corporate power in the city as well as the country. Prince first business of the day was a meeting with Mrs. Jacky Williams, the community affairs leader and representative of the alliance to conserve old Richmond Neighborhoods. It was their second meeting on the subject of residential renovations. While in an adjourning suite, Brother Shabazz was in a meeting of his own with Camelot Resources developer and contractors from Virginia Architect and Contractor. Prince and Shabazz were covering all grounds today. They had lunch with a private developer from Brooklyn, NY. Mr. Jay Hollinsworth who was considering investing 1 million to Black Wall St's million for funding toward Prince's idea of renovating a 300 unit complex that the city of Richmond just happened to also have an interest in. While the city had ideas of a county club with golf courses, with a 10,000 a year fee from its members, Prince had other ideas. He wanted to renovate the area for low income housing where a single tenant could only make 28,000 or less annually to qualify to live there. A house hold of four could earn no more than $40,000. Hollingsworth respected Princes ideas. Another meeting was planned for later in the month. A firm handshake and Prince was off to the next business.

Prince met with community leaders furthering his ideas and winning over more silent investors. Education, employment and athletics were his tools of weaponry to succeed in the fight against his adversaries. So the final business of the day was community service. Prince's project would be backed and supported by Virginia Union University which would provide on and offsite programming. And George Iverson High school would mentor the elementary as well as middle school residents of Prince's housing community. Tenants would be recruited and placed into jobs established by Brother Shabazz and the Richmond career center in the area. Also the I.N. had agreed to host midnight basketball league in an organized and safe environment sponsored by the community affairs leader, Jacky Williams. It was funny how things changed. In his previous life, Prince had held many titles and not all of them positive ones either. But it was a good feeling to really be handling real business because as a young cat working his way up through the ranks, he knew the difference between business and real business… "Young nigga, you ain't got no business…The white man got business, niggas got arrangements."

Glancing down at the hands on his platinum presidential Rolex, a smile touched Prince's lips as he reflected back over the old man's remark nearly 20 years ago. Though a stone cold dope fiend, P. Funk knew what the hell he was talking about. God bless his soul, Prince wished he was alive now to see what had become of the troubled adolescent. His thoughts were interrupted by his intercom speaker, Ms. Brittney; his loyal young secretary was promptly informing her boss that today's business was officially at its end. One last glance out over the city as he was gathering his briefcase, he thought to himself. 'Business is never over; in fact it's just about to begin.' Prince made his way out of the James Center suite toward a waiting elevator joining his partner attorney, Shabazz. They both rode in silence waiting for the city to strike back because the Black Wall St. Enterprise had definitely hit a major lick. The business partners smiled at the thought as they exited the elevator, exchanged hugs, handshakes and pleasantries then parted their separate ways. Shabazz peeled off into the night in his tinted black Escalade and Prince exited the James Center parking lot in his black on Black Maybache, Black Wall St. personalized plates disappeared into the night, Black Wall St. business concluded for the day.

But the game never stops. Two unmarked city vehicles slowly stalked through the night behind each Black Wall St.

executive keeping their distance, but never losing focus of the targeted black luxury vehicles. Prince and Shabazz instinctively glanced through each of their rearview mirrors at approximately the same time noticing the cars tailing them. Each man smiled to himself thinking, yeah the game never stops, indeed.....

Chapter

9

Nat Turner

Everything looked to be on the up and up. Back in the pen when RISING SUN was just a mere thought in my mind, I'd spend countless hours fantasizing about it. Imagining myself as a mighty general leading a strong army of righteous men and women, was I kidding myself. Did I have what it took to handle such a task? And why me, I didn't ask for this, I was chosen….that had to be the case. I always reflect on the dreams I would have in prison…The visions that lead me to this particular point in my life. Many of us lack vision, which is why we as a people are perishing so vehemently. I made a vow to myself that if ever I got a chance to pursue this dream of mine, I'd go hard. So hard, that the impact of this movement would be similar to a violent earthquake. Over the next few months, my schedule would become so hectic that there wouldn't be enough hours in a day to do what I needed to do.

The autobiography was doing incredible, which enabled me to travel and connect with many wonderful people. And it's funny because on the plane one weekend headed out to Chicago, I sat right next to a young lady of European decent, who just happened to have the book in her possession. The entire flight her eyes stayed glued to the pages. Although I was curious of her opinion, anxious to know if she liked or disliked it, I never said a word. I was just satisfied to know that my story had crossed all racial boundaries. But that incident on the plane was just the first of many occurrences. The book couldn't stay on the bookshelves and from the slums to Suburban America; folks seemed to be fascinated with the story, not to mention the Author who wrote it.

By the way, him being a Richmond native, we often got together for lunch or just hung out at some low key spot in the city to discuss the success of the book. The Ghost wasn't your typical author who was obsessed with the lime light or sick with the Hollywood flu, but he was totally the opposite. He said to me once that he never wanted to become so famous that he couldn't enjoy peaceful moments with his family out in public. And that he loved the fact that he could breeze by undetected and blend in with the average Joe. I agreed because at the end of the day, family was everything. The more people read the book, the more folks began to flock to RISING SUN. In California and Saint Louis where Chapters were being set up by appointed representatives, memberships started to increase. More so in the prisons, brothers whom I left behind the wall, were still soldering hard inside and recruiting younger cats as they entered the institution.

In Richmond, progress was definitely being made; speaking engagements was also a plus. We never failed to add on to the count after one of my lectures. The (P.O.P) Foundation was out in the Marcy Community working hard. In a meeting with Kihiem once, I suggested that we start a free lunch program like the Black Panthers did in the 60's. A lot of folks didn't know where such a program originated. Oh that's right; the Government stole the credit for what our brothers had established, just as they had done all our inventions. I told Kihiem that by implementing the program, we could reach more children that way.

In my inner actions with the youngsters, I quickly learned that they weren't bad as some folks made it seem. Like any civilized human being, they simply wanted to be heard and desperately needed to be a part of something. Not only did the free lunch program work, but it strengthened the bond between residents in the neighborhood. And eventually, we added the free lunch program to the other neighborhoods where the (P.O.P) Foundation had already been working. Something wonderful happened around that time. I had just landed into the city from New York. I got a call from Kihiem as I was leaving the airport with Prina behind the wheel. He said that he was down at Ms. Betty Lee's place and needed to see me, emphasizing that it was urgent. Although exhausted from the long flight, I headed straight there. As we arrived within a block of the Marcy neighborhood, it looked nothing like the place I visited almost a year ago. The streets were cleaner than they'd ever been. Grownups sat on their porches sipping ice cold beverages while children ran about freely as if they had not a care in the world. What a sight to see. A child shouldn't have to be burdened with drug deals and shootouts.

I marveled at the adorable girls jumping rope as we pulled up alongside them across from Ms. Betty Lee's house. It had been awhile since I'd seen children being children. But it could be done when strong brothers like the (P.O.P) posted up in the neighborhood. They were there for the duration to build a strong community. I slid out of the truck the moment I spotted Kihiem and a few brothers from the organization. It was about four or five of them all sporting regular street gear, leaning up against company issued SUVs. Kihiem dressed in an oversized crispy white tee shirt, jeans and a fresh pair of buttery Timbs. I focused on him as he came strolling up with this certain mysterious look about him. He gave Prina a shout out, and then we stood at the hood of the truck to talk. With a wide grin stretched across his face, he said "Allah, is the Best of Planners,"

"What," I asked wondering what he meant by it. Then he nodded over to the group and a figure I hadn't recognized until that very moment, emerged and came walking over at us. Shoulder length braids, solid black tee-shirt with sagging Eighty Seven jeans and some black and red Air Jordan's, I winced inside flashing back over that menacing glare...the burner and possibly a bloody murder scene if the old lady hadn't intervened. Immediately, I turned to Kihiem skeptically, like what the hell was this? But he read me.

"Relax Nat, he just wanna rap to you."

I didn't doubt Kihiem, but damn give a brother a heads up next time. I eyed Cory as he approached, studying him for intent....his movements, still half convinced of the purpose behind the surprise visit. And I admit, there was a different look about him, an unmistakable look of humbleness about him. Before when he had run down on me, he appeared as though he'd been demonized of some sort, but now he stood before me innocent like a child. I didn't feel threatened and strangely, this overwhelming feeling of compassion and love for the young man suddenly cut through me. As I figured he would, Corey apologized for his actions and said he was confused that day and that there was no real reason why he acted out in that way. But he was sorry...with tears in his eyes, he went on to say that he wanted to change his life but he didn't know how or where to even begin. Fresh out of juvenile detention, Corey expressed his regards for what had become of his old stomping ground (Marcy Project's). He said it took him six months in juve-hall to actually figure out that a clean neighborhood was really the best alternative for everyone. He hadn't known anything else prior...He always thought that (selling drugs in his own neighborhood) was the way it was supposed be. Corey later said that he only knew of two realities and that was (Prison or a violent death) and he wanted neither.

"Can I be a part of your organization, Sir" Corey asked. "Man I just know it'll make my mama proud."...

Until this day, I still wonder how much involvement Kihiem had in this young man's decision. The more familiar I became with the city of Richmond, the more I learned of how heavily connected and influential Kihiem and Prince were over the city's residents even the youth. I felt fortunate to be a part of that. But I would later learn of a shooting that took place involving one of the Mosques. Kihiem just so happened to be the student Minister there at the time of the Mosque being shot up. Less than 24 hours of the incident taking place, the young man who'd used the Sacred House for target practice, was snuffed out and found dead in the streets. Soldering with the I.N in prison, there was always talk about an army you saw and one you didn't see. The street dwellers and dope pushers, who wouldn't dare join on to the ranks of the Islam Nation but never the less, respected their efforts and would burn any potential threat to the Brothers and their mission. It's never good to lose one of our young brothers, even if he's done something as stupid as shooting up the people's Mosque. And I'm sure if Kihiem could've intervened on the brother's behalf, he would have. So I guess bringing Corey to me was his way of atoning in some way for his pass failures...maybe.

While I'm at it, let me introduce Star, another unique member of the organization. She came to me; well I came to her rather a year or so after my release from prison. In the pen, I'd always visualize myself fallen up in some strip club, not to participate but to search and recruit members. Sounds ridiculous right? It's true, though. After being exposed to the Islam Nation, it was hard to even entertain such thoughts, let alone go through with them. Of course, I never shared those thoughts, plus I didn't believe that I'd ever have the heart to do it. But one night while working late at the office, I was reading over some literature and stumbled over something that would help justify my crazy thinking. In a nut shell, it simply said that in order to reach a people down in the mud as our people were, then it may cause for you to have to go down in the mud and get them...

That was all the confirmation I needed. I glanced up from my reading material and studied my step son for a moment sitting at the desktop computer answering emails. My thoughts sometimes could seem ridiculous to the average person. But never the less, I asked Doug Jr. what he thought. Would he go out with me, I must've sounded like a fool. He responded with surprise just as I thought he would. "Get the hell outta here, you serious man."

"Yeah, don't look at me like that because it's not what you think."

"It ain't. You did say strip club, right."

"Just so you'd know, I got all the woman I need waiting for me at home."

"A strip club with naked hoes...I mean naked women." Doug corrected.

"Are they naked, really?" I said clowning. "You know it's been a while since I've been..."

"Yeah right," Doug said.

We shared a mutual gaze as I went on to say. "Doug look man, your mother is the only woman for me. This here is just business, RISING SUN business."

"Rising Sun business huh? What's more important?"

We both agreed that it was best to leave Prina out of this one. I just so happened to know a guy from down in VA. Beach who threw some of the best dance parties around. With nearly 20 years of experience, Dame was an expert at what he did. But the parties were always exclusive and nothing but heavy hitters and game spitters with special invitations could attend. Everything prearranged and the location was never the same. From the moment Dame heard I'd touch the land, (release from prison) he had been bugging me to attend one of his functions for old time's sake. In my heyday, I would patronize the strip club scene. A night stalker, practically living in the clubs, partying like a rock start but so much had changed since then. Didn't have the stomach for it anymore, Dame called though, said he was in town and wanted to see me later that night at a party he arranged at the Sheraton Hotel.

The scenery was typical, held in a spacious banquet room of a high end hotel. Dame was well known throughout Virginia for his live private parties. The average Joe couldn't just roll up into one of his sets. He had access to all the high rollers and whenever he'd visit a certain area, he'd send out invitations. Ever since we were youngens, trying to come up in the streets of VA, Dame had always kept a fine stable of lovely women. The dope boys loved him for that fact alone and the hotel managers never missed an opportunity to do business with him because Dame made them a fortune. We arrived just in time to hear Dame give his famous speech about respecting the women and not being shy with the cash and then suddenly the music dropped. And out from the mounted in ceiling speakers, came Lil Wayne's (Lick you like a Lollypop). Then through a set of double doors, one by one, beautiful dancers emerged, strutting forward, hips swaying seductively as they filled the room, their luscious lips sucking on lollypop. I thought that was pretty fly.

Dame had definitely stepped his game up. The women were all different flavors now, unlike how it was back in the day when there was just a stable full a cute sister's. But now, he had a variety of different girls for his customers to choose from. From snow bunnies gone wild, to sexy Latinas dancers, they were all dropping it like it's hot. Ball players were in the house tonight. Sofas lined the walls where the guys sat being entertained. Once the cash began to rain, dope boys showing out, garments started to fly in the air.

"Damn," I thought observing the scene from a far. That was me 20 years ago for sure. Making it rain, tossing dead presidents up as if it wasn't a thang. Islam Nation came to mind as I stood there and observed from the bar. The topless women were shaking their naked behinds for a worthless piece of paper that was losing its value every day. But of course it wasn't their fault, for they were simply trying to get ahead the best way they knew how, similar to the dope boys on the street corner. The set wasn't the same for me, I felt out of place. While I sat nursing my non-alcoholic beverage, I noticed how the girls danced for a good 10 to 15 minutes, then rotated with another group of girls. Dame had really up graded his game. By doing it that way, it was more exciting and to, it enabled the girls to really work it, get their cash and be gone, regroup and come back. At least from my observation, that's what I saw. Far too many times before, I'd see dancers over exert themselves only to be disrespected and paid chump change for their hard work. I didn't feel comfortable; it felt as if I was being watched. By who, I could only guess. The last thing I needed was to read about this in the papers. I could hear my critics now, slandering me and spewing all kinds of hypocritical remarks about how in one instance, I claimed to be an advocate for the empowerment of women and the next, degrading them by attending nude bars.

Damn, the very thought gave me a head rush. The second group's time was up as they moved swiftly to collect their belongings and the left over cash that had fallen on the dance floor. I was on my second Red Bull when I turned and was stunned by what I thought was the prettiest, most adorable face in the room. She resembled a black bobby doll. Possibly in her mid 20's about six feet tall in strappy four inch heels, she wore a silver dress with spaghetti straps that hung loosely....suggestively might I add over her tight frame. It was hard not to stare and I had to catch myself. She stepped to the bar, shot me what appeared to be her best smile.

"You buying?" she asked.

"What are you drinking," was my response."

"Grey Goose and cranberry, thank you very much."

"Don't mention it." I said and gestured to the lovely bartender to serve the lady.

"I need a quick pick me up, you know…I'm about to go on any second now."

"Oh, so you're dancing tonight."

"That's right, so you may as well join the fun and stop acting all anti…"

"Me anti...Come on" I responded with a wide grin

"Look at you….you all over here alone while everyone else is enjoying themselves…"

"What makes you think I'm not enjoying myself?" She shot me a quick glance before grabbing her drink, "Yeah right," she said then drained her glass in one take. I notice on her right bicep a very interesting piece of art work that caught my attention. It was a tatted Black widow spider with words under it that read, 'Beautiful but Deadly.' It wouldn't have been right if I didn't inquire about it. It just struck me as odd that someone as lovely as her could be considered deadly. Unless I was simply reading too much into it, so I asked her what was the story behind that tat. What did it mean, if it meant anything at all? There was a brief silence as she paused to acknowledge the artwork as if she was reflecting. I concluded that from the glare she shot me, that I had reopened a wound that she wished had remained shut. Then there was this certain emptiness behind those penetrating eyes that hadn't been there before my poking into her business. Her adorable face suddenly hardened as she looked at me and in that one instant, she appeared much older than what she actually was.

"It means just what it says…gotta a name mister"

"They call me Nat." That beautiful smile was back...

"Well Nat, I'm Star. Appreciate the drink, bye." She started off but paused. "Hey loosen up a little will you." She said before taking off. No sooner had she walked off, my man Dame walked up. Same ol' Dame, still icy and fresh to death in a Velour sweat suit with same Gucci boots on his feet, Vintage Cazal shades covered his eyes.

"Nat you still a freak," Dame stated giving me a pound. "Yeah boy, I caught you checking out my girl. Honey a rare breed. She one of the baddest bitches I got. Ain't nothing change my nigga, your boy still on top of his game. You want that, just say the word...."

Indeed, Dame hadn't missed a beat. He still had his so called pimp game intact. I had to laugh because it had been so long since I'd seen this fool. "No man, I'm good. I see you still doing what you do."

"Well hey a nigga gotta eat. The dope game ain't no game no more..."

"I plead the fifth," I said and we both laughed. My thoughts were so far removed from drugs, selling it at least, that I tried to avoid any conversation pertaining to it. Dame took one look at the Red Bull I'd been sipping on and said. "You don't drink no more either."

"No Dame, I gave it up."

'Well I'll be damned. Nigga I ain't seen you in almost two decades and you telling me you can't even have a drink with you boy...No alcohol, no weed and you ain't even trying to fuck one of these pretty bitches in here...What the hell happened man. What they do to you in prison...laughs...laughs...laughs...

"Get the hell outta here Dame." I said and turned to face him. "It's just not for me no more." I told him as my eyes traveled around the spacious room at all the action. Cash was flying in the air as dancers performed to Usher's "Make love

in the Club." Fleshly body parts glistened in the dimly lit
room. Doug Jr. seemed to be having a ball. I glanced across the
room just in time to see a dancer demonstrate how she could
make her butt cheeks perform a standing ovation.

"A lot can change in 17 years, Dame"

"Yeah...I can dig it playboy. Damn though....17 years?
What the hell happen to all those years?"

"I don't know man, but it's gone and here we are."

"It's good to have you back, though for real. We like the
only two left out here. Yo, I read the book"

"And...you like it or not."

"Like it, the joint official. I mean straight up off the chain,
the realest shit I ever read. But Nat let me ask you something.
The shit that happen to you in prison, was that Real Talk."

"Every word of it," I answered not batting an eye. He
threw an arm over my shoulder and said that he was proud of
me. We talked for a few more minutes until he had to jet off to
attend to other business. I saw Star once more before the night
had ended. For some reason that I couldn't quite put a finger
on, I found myself drawn to her in some crazy way. I wrapped
her up for a few minutes in conversation about my organization, which she knew nothing about. And she didn't care to
know anything either. But of course, she was at work and I
understood so for the little time I held her up, I compensated
her with a couple hundred bucks and a business card. Then I
thanked her for her time and said that if she wanted to know
more, give me a call. It would be two months later before Star
and I would cross paths again but unfortunately, our meeting
this time would take place under entirely differently circumstances. There was a disturbing message left on my voicemail
from Star, saying that she was in a jam and that I was the only

person in the world who she felt she could call on. She had been arrested in Prince George County for assault with a deadly weapon after leaving a stranger's party where she'd been approached by an overly aggressive customer who'd been stalking her the whole night. The loony white guy wanted more than what the dancer was willing to offer and when Star showed defiance, he literally tried to strong arm her. But in the nick of time, Star was able to retrieve the hidden razor she kept concealed under her tongue. Star delivered over a dozen painful sharp lashes across the man's arm and face with it, sending her attacker bailing for help.

In spite of her plea of acting in self defense, she was arrested and booked by Prince George County police for acting out too aggressively. Who in the hell cared about a stripper anyway... I did...I didn't waste a second in bailing her out on $15,000 bail. On the drive back to the city, we stopped and I bought her lunch at Applebee's restaurant. After listening to her give me the spill on what had happened to her the night before, I asked her did she like her occupation....Being a stripper and all.

"No not really," she replied with a distasted expression that confirmed what she really felt.

"Then why do it, then"

"It pays the bills." She chewed her food slowly as if she was contemplating over something, then she looked over at me. "Have you ever done something you don't necessarily like doing, but you do it anyway because you feel you have to."

"Yeah of course, but"-

"So there you have it," she cut me off. "Imagine being a 24 year old single mother of two children. None of their daddy's helps me, and I can't get a good job because I lack the qualified education. It's hard as hell being out here alone. And If I don't have money, my babies won't be able to eat and I'll be damned if I let mines go without. So if I gotta dance, and shake my ass to survive, then so be it."

The tattoo on her arm drew me in again as she spoke. And I must've been reckless eye balling because she caught me staring and with her other hand, she self consciously covered the tattoo. She looked across the table at me, shaking her head as her eyes begin to cloud with tears. "Nat you don't know what's it's like..."She managed a painful smile as tears trickled down both sides of her cheek. "You'll never know what it's like to be me."

Star didn't reveal to me that day that she'd been previously infected with HIV over a year ago. We never lost contact again and eventually, she broke down and told me the story behind the tattoo on her arm. She was indeed beautiful but she had been infected with a deadly disease. By this time, she was somewhat familiar with the organization from reading newspaper articles and I had given her an autograph copy of my book. Over the next couple of months, she started to show interest in the movement. She asked questions and soon began to show a desire for change. I would drill in to her head that life for her didn't have to be over. In prison, I learned from participating in AID AWARENESS classes, that a victim living with the virus could live a normal life if they received treatment in time. But the medication was expensive and Star was barely getting by. I really wanted to help this sister; I even talk to Prina about her. There ain't nothing like having a strong woman by your side. I had given this thing a lot of thought and yet, I still seemed to come up with nothing. I kept asking myself how she could contribute to the organization, a secretary job maybe. But in one take, Prina nailed it. She said that Star could be an Advocate for her disease. She went on to say that she should speak out and share her experience to help other young women like herself and possibly benefit financially as well. She was smart enough and very articulate. All she needed was to be thoroughly educated about her disease and I would provide her with all the necessary information. Lastly, I would have to convince her to share herself with the world. Unlock the chains and come out of the mental prison that she'd built for herself. It took a while but she eventually did. "It's not about you no more," I'd often say to her. Now she had the opportunity to not only live to see her children grow, but she could inspire hope in others. I wasn't in a position to save the world; however with the many blessings given to me, it was only right that I share them with others in need.

Star admitted finally that she needed help. I assisted her with lawyer fees. The guy who'd assaulted her, we contacted his attorney and threatened to press attempted rape charges against his client if he didn't drop the charges against Star. The man had a family and he worked security at a prestigious bank in the County. We pressed to file a report and go public about it and blow him up in the tiny Prince George County if he didn't break. And he did, eventually about two weeks before their court appearance. Star was grateful and she never danced again after that. There were too many risks involved and God forbid, if something happened to her, her children would have no one. That thought alone was enough to change her mind. She enrolled in AIDs Awareness classes to learn more about her virus. We visited doctors who spoke to her about different medications. I let her accompany me on some of my trips where I would lecture to over hundreds of college students. Star caught on fast. Once she conquered her fears and learned how to keep her emotions intact, the girl handled the podium as one who had been doing it for years. When she spoke, there would be people in the audience shedding tears. It was unreal. She gave me so much inspiration just knowing how far she'd come. From swinging on stripper poles to now standing before hundreds of people as a motivational speaker. She went from being paid by me to setting her own fee to speak about her condition. By this point there wasn't anything she didn't know about the virus she'd been infected with, she could now earn enough money to provide for her family as well as buy the medication she needed to stay alive. And the most important thing of all, instead of degrading herself to do it, she was giving hope to a lot of women like herself... you couldn't beat that with a bat.

Chapter

10

Assata Shakur Muhammad, daughter to Kihiem and his lovely wife Pearl, Assata was the manifestation of what true education could do if applied properly. At the mere age of 8, she was bilingual, speaking Arabic and Spanish fluently and not only that, but she had read both Koran and Bible from cover to cover and could recite biblical scripture as good as the average grown up. She was also a chest player and had a passion for writing poetry. In fact, she'd recently completed a poetry book chosen for display in the city's Museum. She was a home schooled child. Pearl refused to enroll her daughter into the Richmond public school system which she often referred to as the killing field for their children.

She had lost all faith in the system. Because of the home schooling and extra love and attention, Assata advanced tremendously and was so far ahead of students in her age group that even if she were to be enrolled in public schools, she'd most certainly have to be skipped up a couple grades. Kihiem was so impressed with his daughter's accomplishments and how quickly she was progressing. But he couldn't take the credit, Pearl took on many roles, ensuring that Assata get everything she needed. The name Assata means (She Who

Struggles.) The idea to give their daughter such a name came from the legendary Mother Panther, Assata Shakur, who over three decades ago, escaped a falsified prison sentence and had to flee for her life to Cuba where she remained in exile up until this present day. Kihiem had read all about her in prison and had come to really have a genuine love for her. He was so taken by her courageous spirit that he vowed that when and if he ever had a little girl, he would give her the name of such a brave soul.

Parking the spacey F-150 pickup truck in the drive way of their cozy three bedroom tri level home right off of Laburnum Avenue, Kihiem cursed under his brief noticing that the light inside Assata's bedroom was off. It was the second time this week that he missed tucking her in. One day she'd be old enough to understand that daddy was only trying to make a better world for her. Sometimes he felt he had the hardest job in the world. There were problems on top of problems in the Ghetto. Teen pregnancy, drug addiction and self hatred were like a cancer corroding away at the people souls. Hope was lost, sort of like looking at life through the rearview mirror. From their perspective, they just couldn't see things getting better. Admittedly, going into these Projects talking clean up wasn't a walk in the park. In fact, it was the most difficult challenge, not to mention the craziest shit that he'd ever done. But never the less, someone had to do it. And why not him, when he'd done so much evil in the past. It seemed as though God was making him revisit his past and try to correct it. So many lives had been exterminated during his infamous days of running with his gang, (The Juice Crew.)

Was he really doing God's will or was he simply a vicious, cold blooded monster to sit before Ms. Betty Lee, knowing that it was his sinful hands that had brought the old lady's boys to a naught. He wondered about that sometimes. The past was never lost in his memory and he could recall the 80's turf wars so vividly. Ms. Betty Lee's sons...The Juice crew had been rivals as far back as junior high. Chaz, Brock and Red, their names held heavy weight back in those days and that's not referring to dumbbells either. Rappers talked a good game but these brothers were real life duffle bag boys. But while they were living flamboyant life styles, pushing the hottest whips, sporting the flyest dime sexes around their arms, The Juice Crew were playing chest, plotting and strategically setting up to get rid of the opposition. Brock and Red were the muscle of the three so Kihiem, "Justice", at that time rather, baited them in with his twin Lugers that he brought down from Jersey.

Cindy and Angel...these girls were so gorgeous that immediately upon seeing them, their beauty could not be denied. Philippine mixed with black, Angel had long flowing jet black hair that reached the small of her back, dark brown skin, slanted eyes and a cute face and a body that spoke volumes. And Cindy was a younger version of the lovely Stacey Dash with a nice petite frame and those same alluring eyes. At first sight of the girls, the brothers Red and Brock bit the bait. Not even 24 hours later, the girls had gotten the brothers so far out of their element, that they dropped their guard. Justice at the time was right there to capitalize. The brothers never knew what hit them. Justice, a name given to him by his peers because of his precise and unconscionable style to serve street justice, he shot them both dead. Cindy and Angel were sent back up Jersey and six months later, The Juice Crew caught Chase, duck-taped him and manage to make him cough up nearly a million in cash before sending him off to be with his

brothers. Almost six years later after Justice had been convicted and sent to prison, he received word that Cindy and
Angel was found strangled to death in a hotel room in Los
Angeles. Their deaths weren't related to The Juice Crew, the
girls were pros at what they did, moving from state to state,
preying on suckers who allowed their little heads to do their
thinking...Somewhere along the line, the girls had obviously
met with some back luck.

It wasn't easy to live with such demons and judging from
the man he became, Justice...the gun slinger...the self annihi-
lator, that beast had long been buried. Nothing happened
without the permissive will of the Most High. And for him to
still be alive after what he'd endured from the street wars and
to serve 18 straight years in confinement, surely his life meant
something. There wasn't a day that went by that he didn't try
to offer a kind word or give service to someone. What happened to Ms. Betty Lee's boys was over and done and could
never be reversed. She would never know how and who was
responsible and for what purpose did she need to know
anyway. Black Wall St was the business at hand. There was
nothing more important at this point and time then cleaning
up the neighborhoods and taking back economic power.

Speaking of which, 5 years ago, there were over a dozen
Korean owned Beauty Supply stores. These business owners
targeted black communities, sucking the blood out of the poor
and giving nothing back. Black Wall St's coming changed all
of that. Kihiem, Reverend Rodney and other community
leaders and Black Wall St. affiliates went into the neighborhoods and talked about the exploitation of them by these
foreigners who took from their pockets and gave nothing
back. The mission was broken down and explained to the

residents and they admitted that it made lots of sense that of all the black dollars the Koreans accumulated from their dealings within the Urban Neighborhoods, that they should be generous enough to give something back...Anything, but they could care less, which was not on them to give in the first place.

It should never have been allowed to happen so long anyhow, so the Black Wall St. establishment with the help of the community, set out to run the foreigners out of business. The Manufacturers didn't want to cut anyone other than their own in on the action. So what Black Wall St. did, was boycott their businesses, each and every single one of them until they got the point. Once the residents understood the importance of what was taking place, they followed suit and businesses for the foreigners suddenly started to dwindle. Boycotts were advertised on flyers, the radio even. The movement was so strong that eventually, the Manufacturers folded and invited Black Wall St. to the negotiating table. They were somehow under the silly impression that if they cut Black Wall St. in and distribute goods to them for the same retail price as they did their brothers, that everything would be fine...business could continue to go on as it had been. But what they had failed to comprehend was that Black Wall St's sole objective was to push them out, shut their asses down... *Black Self Owned Beauty Supply Stores* was the plan to cater to the needs of their own people. There wasn't enough room for the foreigners and The Black Wall St. establishment in the city. Either they supply the (Black-owned) stores and continue to prosper, or lose money because the boycotts wouldn't stop....

Fast forward....five years later; there are only twenty beauty supply stores in the city with all but two of them being

Black owned. Black Wall St. had done exactly what it had set out to do, which was to get rid of the ungrateful blood suckers. The foreigners were jumping ship and moving out, possibly to some other vulnerable poor community where they could exploit the people. This wasn't at all a smooth ride, it was like pulling teeth to try and get black folks to get up off their lazy behinds and stand up for something. They had grown so content with being robbed and could give a rat's ass about keeping the money circulating in their own community. But someone had to pick up the torch light and show the Richmond citizens what unity and dedication could bring about.

Black Wall St. picked up that torch. But at the end of the day, after a long hard day's work, what Kihiem valued the most was the comfort of coming home to enjoy a peaceful moment with his family. Pearl hadn't too long gotten out of the bath tub when Kihiem shut the front door behind him and followed her invigorating, sweet fragrance up to their bedroom where she was seated on the edge of the bed. Feeling his strong presence, she lifted her head and found her handsome husband there in the doorway, his engaging stare fixated on her. She flushed inside like a child, while a smile as bright and beautiful as the shining sun suddenly stretched wide across her face. "Hey there," she greeted happily and said, "it's about time you made it home, I was beginning to worry." Pearl voiced in concern. "I missed you."

Kihiem kept his same position for a few seconds more. Pearl was never one to wear clothes that revealed her shapely, well kept physique, so whenever Kihiem caught his wife nude, he was always amazed at how wonderful she looked. She exercised regularly and never missed her regular manicure and pedicure appointments. He eyed her suggestively, drinking in her remarkable smooth ebony brown skin. 'God, what a blessing,' he thought. "You like a breath of fresh air woman."

"Am I really," she said blushing from ear to ear.

"Yes baby, you are."

"Well come on over here and show me some love." She gestured to her cosmetic chest where she kept all her good smelling Victoria Secret lotions and oils. "You're just in time."

In the confines of their bedroom, Alicia Key's soothing voice played softly while Kihiem's skillful hands worked magically against his wife's flesh. Nothing seemed to escape them in conversation. Kihiem expressed guilt for another night coming in late. But as usual, Pearl understood, she knew his line of work caused for him to be away. Besides, it wasn't like he was running the streets like a dog chasing tail. Personal feelings aside, she had to do all that she possibly could to support him. And she would always reassure him not to be sorry for something that God had described for him to do. Aside from (God), Pearl was his biggest inspiration. She gave him encouragement and would often say to him that he was a good husband as well as father. And that every day she seemed to fall more in love with him because of his sincere efforts to exemplify Allah in his daily actions. That so turned her on. She was grateful but she'd put in the work too. They say good things come to those who wait...Well Pearl waited 18 years for her good man. She was a natural.

"Wanda's in town, she flew in today from Atlanta." Pearl said as she slid into her favorite Donna Karen negligee.

"Really, I didn't know she was back."

"We supposed do brunch tomorrow."

Kihiem was listening as he stripped down to his boxer shorts. Wanda was Princes wife of more than fifth teen years. She was his Bonnie...his ride a die chick, Wanda spent a lot of time back and forth between Atlanta and Richmond, tending to various business ventures. Black Wall St's first lady was just as shrewd as her husband when it came to regulating business deals. She had been taught by the best.

"Honey, I love this book," Pearl expressed excitedly as she retrieved Nat's autobiography from a nearby night stand, eager to get back in it.

"You haven't finish reading that book yet woman," Kihiem questioned and fell in beside her in their spacious king size bed. "It shouldn't take a person two months to read a book."

"Yeah I know right...but wait, it hasn't been two months either Kihiem. Maybe a month in a half," she added with a cute smile.

"Is there a difference?" Kihiem was being cynical

"But you're right, I guess. I could've been finished. It's just so intriguing that I don't wanna finish..." She turned to him. "Don't you just hate that?"

"Not really."

Pearl mushed his head playfully, knowing that he was simply being his typical funny self. "But you read it right, what did you think?"

"Oh, I thought the book was real good. It's a good read...powerful."

"So what is he like?"

"Who Nat?"

"Yeah who else, Kihiem. What do you think about him? It just seems like you two are really close. Aside from the Brotherhood and Prince and Jeffrey maybe, I've never seen you take to anyone like that before."

Kihiem took a moment to ponder over his wife's words then he came with his reply. "I respect his mind. And I believe that he was sent by Allah. His movement is strong. Young people are clinging to it like magnets. I'm talking brothers who wouldn't come near the Islam Nation, is joining on with this brother...And that's a good thing because we're all one anyway." Kihiem was about to go on before noticing on Pearl's face, that all too familiar expression when she had something on her mind that she wanted to express. "Okay I'm listening," Kihiem said.

Pearl laughed, "Listening, how you figure I got something to say."

"Yeah right, I know that look, now spill."

"It's nothing really," she faced her husband. "It's just that I got the impression from my conversation with Wanda yesterday, that Prince had a different perspective."

"And how did you get at that. Did Wanda say something?"

"No, not really, it's just a vibe I felt when I mention Nat's book. It just struck me as odd that neither she, nor Prince had read it."

Kihiem smiled inside. He really wanted to laugh because Prince was a funny cat. Prince had read Nat's autobiography first, before Kihiem even so his telling Wanda he didn't read it was beyond his comprehension. But that was simply Prince's unorthodox way of doing things. His actions at times could be confusing as hell but never vain...

"So..." Pearl continued to probe, "I'm I close..."

"Yeah baby you hit it on the nail. Unfortunately, Prince doesn't share my feelings about brother Nat. You know the man got serious trust issues."

"You can't really blame him for that, now can you."

"No baby, I don't suppose I can. He's just being his cautious self but this situation with Nat, I'd have to differ with my brother. Look, because the man's organization has gained legs and is growing fast every day, to Prince it gotta be a trick or something to it."

"What do you mean, I'm not following you," Pearl voiced puzzled.

"My point exactly, there ain't nothing to get. I don't know, maybe Prince feels like with all the work we've put in over the years to get to the level we're at and then Nat comes straight out of prison with virtually no obstacles in his way and have everything handed to him on a silver platter."

"Like a fairytale or something, huh." Pearl said.

"Exactly, but I don't agree with that."

"Well, we know just from reading his book that he paid a price."

"And to baby, the brother had a plan and now, he's simply executing it. Nat is cleaning brothers and sisters up and giving them jobs. And with his own money too, might I add. Just look at what he did for that young lady."

"Yeah Star right. "Pearl replied. "We met last week. She's a nice girl."

"And see, that right there is a prime example of how wonderful this guy is. I really love that brother for what he did for that girl. We're all moving in the same direction, I just don't understand, we should embrace a brother like that...Feel me..."

"Of course I do sweetheart. But let's not discard what Prince is saying either. He didn't make it this far by being a fool. Obviously, there's some logic behind his thinking. Prince is just being cautious and he has every right to be. For as long as I have known him, he's always been this way and this situation is nothing new." Pearl laughed… "Prince is just being Prince." She fixed her gaze on Kihiem. "You know your brother."

"Yeah maybe you're right," Kihiem admitted. "But you know for some reason, whenever I think about RISING SUN, my father's words come to mind… "There's nothing more powerful than an idea whose time has come." Kihiem breathed a deep sigh, staring up at the ceiling at nothing.

"The idea of unity amongst the street organizations, not gangs. I gotta stop using that term, any group of people nowadays can be labeled as a gang. But the idea of peace between them has come, which is why RISING SUN is having so much success. Kihiem shook his head and continued. "Prince doesn't understand."

"He will baby," Pearl said as she cuddled up beside Kihiem. "Sooner or later, Prince will come around." Her soft tender lips rained steamy wet kisses along his neck and chin. "Just give him a little time….Now enough of talk about Prince okay and Nat and RISING SUN…hug me damn it!!

Chapter

11

Nat Turner

The summer was bearing down, which I thought was perfect timing for the new gymnasium to have its Grand Opening. We spent the entire winter remodeling and perfecting the building so that, come summer time, the hard head youngsters would have a place where they could escape the heat. It was nothing as extravagant as what Prince and brother Kihiem had set up with the Youth Center, but it was a start. Plus, my money and resources weren't as strong; however I was making smart business investments with the little I had. But with the new gym, I was doing something slightly different. Jimmy, my coordinator as well as the best and only boxing trainer in the city, I connected with this brother to assist me in running the center. In his mid 50's with over 30 years of experience, the old man still had a passion for the sport. His youngest boy, Joseph was a professional brawler. In the Welter Weight Division, the guy had squared off with some of the fierce gloves in the business. And he gave me his word that he'd stop by the gym every once in a while to give the kids some inspiration. Aside from getting the gym up and running, I was bouncing back and forth from the Cap City to New York. Recently, I accompanied a small congregation from the Civil Rights community at a press conference in Brooklyn NY, where I spoke about the need for RISING SUN to grow into a universal movement. There at the press conference, I met with rival gangs who personally admitted that the things they had in common were more important than their differences. No matter what city or state I visited, it was the same old sad story. Devastated mothers whose sons had been victims of senseless violence, stood huddled together in solidarity at the rallies that I'd attend. They wore portrait T-shirts of the deceased and some held posters high in the air of their young faces. In the audience, as I would speak to them, I could feel the pulse of their pain, if as though we shared the same nervous system. Their saddened eyes would glisten with anticipation as I would talk about the possibilities of ending gang violence through the new organization. And they were with me. At the end of the rallies, the women would greet me with hugs of appreciation. They'd ask me how they could assist the organization. My support system was growing every day.

Celebrities and entertainers who didn't want to be directly involved, they'd simply let their cash do the talking. Many of them had friends and family members who were up to their necks in crime. And simply put, these street cats were gonna make ends meet somehow. Whether it was selling poison or getting it the Ski Mask way (stick ups). But if we could create a new image in the hood and invest in the kind of resources and intervention programs so that young people could see that joining a gang wasn't their only alternative. I didn't want to spread myself too thin, but so many folks were calling for us. There were a number of organizations doing good work, but nothing like RISING SUN. No organization had reached out solely to the gang problem. I've said many times before that with the right guidance, these same guys could do a lot of good. With unity, we become a Brotherhood and once we establish a Brotherhood, we all become RISING SUNS. I ended a lecture on a similar note as I was preparing to return back to Virginia.

I had received some disturbing news from the main branch in Richmond that caused me to have to cut my short trip short. With the tremendous success we were having with the increase in memberships nationwide, I knew that it was just a matter of time for something to go wrong. It wasn't enough for the Police Gang to discriminate, brutalize and shoot down out right, young black men for sport all across the country...Spilling our precious black blood in the streets without retribution. Wasn't enough...and now, they were after our babies.

Debra Simms seven year old daughter, Senija reportedly had disrupted the classroom in what they labeled as a temper tantrum. She was removed and detained. Not by the teacher or the school's principle, but by the police. That's right, this seven year old child had a set of cuffs slapped around her tiny wrist and had to remain that way until her mother's arrival. But little Senija had cried so hysterically for her mother's rescue, that the poor thing cried herself into a seizure...What the hell good are we if we can't even protect our children? I heard the news and dropped everything and caught the first flight out of New York to go and be by Debra's side. One of the very first people to join us and help out in the beginning stages of RISING SUN, it was only fair that we aided her.

By this time, we had over 50 members in Richmond alone, so upon my arrival at the Emergency Center where Senija was being treated, the waiting area was filled to the capacity with members of the organization. And they were angry as hell. Prina rushed me the moment I entered the room. She fell into my arms and instantly began her revelation of what went down. She led me across the room where Debra sat surrounded by a host of family and friends. She stood as I approached and I embraced her, ensuring her that she wasn't alone. There were family members present, but Senija's dad was in prison serving a long sentence. While I was there, the doctor came in and informed Debra that her daughter was stable and doing much better. Thank God. Once I heard that, it was off to the police precinct to check on a few of the guys who had taken Senija's incident to heart. I prayed that the situation didn't escalate into drama. My brothers were too emotional to think rationally and I didn't want them to give the police a stick to beat them with. But when I arrived, Brother Kihiem and the Islam Nation were there along with RISING SUN warriors.

The environment was controlled and although frustration was easily seen on the brother's faces, they manage to conduct themselves in an orderly fashion. Reverend Rodney Patterson from United Methodist Church was also among the group. He had one of the largest congregations in the city. And I could see why so many people came out to listen. He was a fiery preacher, a real truth spitter. Reverend Rodney Patterson was tied in with the Black Wall St. establishment. I admired him because unlike a lot of bias preachers who brought into the Medias false idealism of painting other religious sects as the enemy, Reverend Rodney Patterson was wise enough to see through their façade. After listening to him preach a sermon one Sunday, he said to me over dinner, that if our leaders would just unite, the people would follow. He went on to add that in many cases, it was our own stubborn leaders who stood in the way of our salvation. And that is why he and the Muslim community decided to come together. I agreed with that concept whole heartedly. It didn't matter that Debra Simms wasn't a member of the preacher's congregation, or affiliated with the Islam Nation, in my absence, the Reverend and Brother Kihiem was there to file a complaint against the officer's reckless act.

A seven year old in handcuffs...Get the hell out of here. And what if she didn't recover from her seizure, which was a direct result of being restrained in that manner. It was a scary thought. Imagine that innocent baby and how devastating it must've been for her to go through something like that. His actions were excessive and uncalled for. Most certainly, he would be held accountable. We were gonna file a lawsuit. Once Senija was back in her mother's custody, everyone departed. It felt good to be a part of a tight knitted community. We had to stop thinking in terms of individualism, because truth be told, we were nothing without one another. Together we stand, divided fall. Leaving the hospital, Prina and I headed straight home. I was exhausted from the long flight and a little frustrated. But I wasn't beat enough to not notice how incredibly pretty my woman looked. Sunk comfortably in the passenger seat while we cruised through the clear night downtown traffic, it seemed like ages since I'd enjoyed the pleasant sight of her lovely face. She let out a pleasurable moan as I began to massage and caress the back of her neck. Then as she stopped for a red light, I tilted her head toward mines and gave her a kiss. It was deep and slow, one that left her stunned and her foot stuck on the brake long after the light had turned green. She casted a curious smirk at me as she hit the gas pedal and the big SUV floored. Every moment that I had spent away from her during my New York trip was now affecting me in a major way. Her luscious full lips glistened in the semi darkness and unconsciously, I licked mines while eyeing her in a lustful fixation. She caught me…damn.

Prina laughed, looked at me and said, "Nat what has gotten into you." She was beaming.

I told her straight faced, "baby you have gotten into me. And when we get home…." It's no need to go there, but best believe, she knows what it is. Her man's in dire need of some intense sexual healing. I just wanted to hold her in my strong arms and kiss her and love her. She was my best friend. We made passionate love that night long into the wee hours of the morning. It was great but something else happen too. Suddenly out of nowhere, her warm tears started to trickle down my chest where her head laid. I felt it and when I attempted to shift her to see what the hell was happening, she just held on to me tighter.

"Can you just please hold me," she pleaded. "I just need you to hold me, Nat, can you do that?"

Of course I did as she wished. Somehow I was beginning to wonder if there was something deeper behind those tears than just good love making…

Chapter

12

On the Eastside of town, Prince was busy holding court of his own. Apparently as he cruised through the Fair Hill Projects, he noticed that a few seeds that had been earlier planted, had been purposely dug up and scattered into the street. Rosetta st. had been the soil of the first seed planted and obviously the first to produce a negative growth. Only one way to salvage the good fruits and that is to destroy the rotten. Tucked low behind the dark tint of a Benz G Wagon, Prince viewed a few familiar faces on post as well as some others he didn't recognize. And what he saw brought him to instant anger. The scenery was all too familiar.... These bastards were slanging dope. The silver truck he was in was fairly new so no one knew who he was although the guys out there desperately tried to look inside.

Every once in a while, Prince would make occasional visits to the city unannounced like today. And though he was a lover of his people, he wasn't at all naïve to the fact that some of those bastards were just downright evil. So for that very reason alone, he took caution in his travels. Accompanying him was his two human bullet Proof Vest. Literally speaking...his two adopted sons, David and Hot Rod never left his side and wouldn't hesitate to take one for their man. They loved Prince. When they were just the mere ages of 14 and 15 years old, Prince being a the close friend of their pops, Big Weed who went down with the Juice Crew back in the day, he took his boys in as though they were his own. With dad doing life and a mom sprung out on crack, it didn't take a rocket a scientist to figure out what direction the boys would head in. From the concrete walls, the Juice Crew member pleaded with his good friend to catch his boys before their curious minds lead them down an unfriendly path of unimaginable heartache and pain... If there was one thing in the world that Prince valued most....it was his word. He didn't bend it or compromise it for nothing or no one. Because of his loyalty, David and Hot Rod never got to taste the street life. At a young age, Prince instilled in the two entrepreneur spirits and told them that when and if they ever went to college, don't be like the clowns who go through four years of schooling, get a degree only to come back home and use their skills to fill another man's pockets with green.

The boys did graduate and eventually, they enrolled in Community College but disaster struck during their second year. Prince was gunned down; barely escaping what was meant to be his death. It was only by the grace of God that he survived such an attack. And ever since that incident, all David and Hot Rod wanted to do was to protect their father. They completed the college courses, received their honorary degrees and returned home to assist Prince in building his empire. Both of them were license and well trained gun handlers. They took their job seriously, making frequent visits to the gun range. To them, Prince was like President Barrack Obama and they were the Secret Service. It was an honor to protect such a man and if need be, they were ready to die in the process...

The cell phone chimed as David came to a stop at 23st and Rosetta. On the other line, it was Prince's ear to the street, a cat name Dip from the Fair Hill Projects just three minutes away.

"Yo P, heard you was out making rounds," said Dip through the phone.

"Yeah D, I'm out and about but Fair Hill not looking to good to my eyes though."

"I already know man. Those cats you just saw... them fools from Garden Central around the corner. Apparently they don't know what's good."

"They don't know what's good," Prince reiterated solemnly as his chest commenced to mount with anger. "Dip I don't wanna hear that shit from you. You know what's at stake and anybody with any sense knows goddamn well what the business is out here and that goes for them muther fuckers I just saw... Look man, dig... this is your area right."

"Right P."

"Well show up around here in a minute and offer these young cats their lives back. We not gone play no games ... they either accept the lives their momma's gave them or they lose it by night fall."

In the front seat, David and his brother, Hot Rod exchange uneasy stares at Prince's last remark. A still silence swept over the truck as he ended the call. In that quick instant, Prince admitted to himself that he'd lost his cool and under no circumstances was that supposed to happen. What the hell had he just done? **A Grave Error!** He knew it...could feel it right in the core of his freaking gut and the damn thing ate away at him like a thousand little piss ant maggots. Prince shook his head…sighed while looking down at his cell phone. So much was at stake and just one careless; bullshit move could cost him everything that he'd work so hard to get. Every one made mistakes right. And even a Prince could slip up….right. **Wrong!** Prince had ordered a foolish hit. This wasn't the 80's when he could knock off a sucker and keep it moving. Talk reckless over an open line and not worry about repercussions. Damn it, this was the technology age and if Dip followed through on such a sinister threat and the wrong ear was eave dropping…

Prince hurriedly punched in Dip's number on his cell and waited for him to pick up. "Yo P," Dip spoke." Somehow I knew you'd call back. What's good my brother."

"About what I said before hanging up… I just wanted to make sure you didn't take me serious." Prince laughed. "You know your man can be a comedian at times."

"No doubt, you can definitely be a jokester when you wanna be. But on a more serious note though, I'm glad as hell you called back. And don't even sweat that situation; because I'm gonna handle that with the best of intelligence."

"Well good, that's what I need to hear. Let me know aight." Prince hung up the phone and exhaled in relief. Focusing his attention on David and Hot Rod, he said "Did you two hear that," Prince asked catching David's eye peering at him through the rear view mirror. "We'll let that be a lesson to the both of you," he went on. "Never conduct business or make important decisions out of anger or emotion."

The next morning, Prince was awakened by the startling voice of his wife. Wanda nudged him hard and said, "It's Kihiem, baby get up." she put the phone to his ear. It was an early Saturday morning, just half past 6am. Prince was dog tired from the night before in which he only got a few hours of shut eye. "Brother this shit better be important," he barked into the receiver, his eyes still half shut.

"Did you catch the news," was Kihiem's only reply then the phone suddenly went dead in Prince's ear. It took a minute for Kihiem's words to register before he became alive. As he passes the phone back to Wanda, slowly regaining his focus, he thought about his favorite slogan. "A Princes work is never done." Turning over in bed, he grabbed the TV remote and turned it on just in time for the channel 12 news. Wanda's soft body cuddled tenderly up under him, igniting an electrifying sensation that shot straight through him. He thought, 'why the hell didn't he just tell me about the news instead of having him sitting up in bed at 6 o'clock in the morning with a bona fide hard on. Right now, I could be making sweet love to my wife ...' Prince was pondering over those thoughts as the Egyptian cotton bed spread rolled up revealing a potion of Wanda's meaty thighs. Then just as he was about to try and reach Kihiem, headlines... **MULTIPLE SHOOTINGS LAST NIGHT,** flashed across the TV screen.

THREE FATAL SHOOTINGS, He was wide awake now. The murders had taken place in the Fair Hill Housing Projects...his territory. Prince waited for 15 minutes watching the news, switching back and forth between channel 8 and 12 news. A news anchor was reporting from the murder scene. Prince stared into the TV, his cheeks trembling with fear. It couldn't be...but it was because he sat in bed dumb founded, taking in the disaster in which had possibly come as a result of a thoughtless act on his part. At any rate, this wasn't a good look. There hadn't been a murder in Fair Hill since the (P.O.P) Foundations intervention. Wanda had awakened by this point and could easily sense trouble just by observing his mood change. They had been soul mates for so long that she knew when something was out of sync. He told her about the homicides, but that was as far as he'd go. It was still a chance that this incident had nothing to do with his discussion with Dip yesterday. God he wished...

"I'll handle it with the best of intelligence." He thought of Dips last words to him. Prince didn't want to believe that homicide was Dips idea of intelligence. Dip had been a loyal soldier for him for years. This wasn't his style but damn... "Did I make myself clear enough"...Prince wondered. His mind raced, desperately hoping that it wasn't what he suspected. Hoping the young cats had taken the warning without protest, because Prince didn't really want that blood on his hands.

Though the rotten fruit had to be destroyed, he was always hopeful that his influence and calculative decision making would prevail over the use of his gun. And on most days they would. But sadly though, what took place on those other days was just the thing Black Wall St. was at war against. Yet even in war, Prince couldn't waver. Three lives had been lost last night...But it was over and done. There weren't no coming back from that shit... Regrets were something he had learned to live with. But it was back to business as usual, Black Wall St business. He had to remain focused on the movement...the big picture.

Chapter

13

Nat Turner

I t all happened so fast. I didn't even see it coming. A late night at the office, I tried to double up on some work so that tomorrow when I came in; the load wouldn't be as heavy. But they'd been watching, waiting and plotting on me...Who? Assassins, extortionist maybe; Lynch Mob types or possibly the real deal...Gangsta Cops, I had not the slightest idea. It was two of them though, camping out under my truck waiting for the perfect opportunity. And when I finally did show, I got as far as the driver's door, when I heard the Mossberg shot gun crack at my dome.

"Don't Fuckin Move," came the violent demand from behind me. But moving wasn't even a thought. My body stiffened, I stood paralyzed. Another figure emerged from out of nowhere... he was hidden under my truck, I was sure of it. Draped in camouflage, black as the dreary night, ski masked up, big gun in hand, he threw a bag over my head and leveled me down to the ground with his gun. Excruciating pain exploded in my head as I collided with the hard concrete. I saw total darkness. I was out of it, slipping in and out of consciousness. I could make out voices...the noisy screech of car tires pulling up. Possibly it was the imaginary vehicle I couldn't see, I reckon. I got the worse fucking luck in the world. This type of madness wasn't supposed to happen to me. In my past life, when I was flying birds from state to state, I stayed on high alert from vouchers like these. Once again, I found myself in a bind, as helpless as a little child. I had to call on the Most High. Who the hell else could I call on in such a time? If it was His will for me to breathe my last breath, then so be it. I put everything in his hands.

I was totally unaware of my location or how much time had passed when I finally regained consciences. My mouth had been ducked taped shut, hands and feet were bound, hog tie style and my head hurt like a son ova bitch! Under the circumstances, I'm sure you can understand my profanity. I was mad as hell. But I was still alive, which was no doubt a good sign that I could remain that way...maybe. It took a couple seconds for my eyes to adjust to the dim room. I focused. There was no furniture, no windows, just a shabby ass room with a door. Where the hell was I? Then a telephone materialized right there in front of me. Unexpectedly, one of the masked men emerged swiftly and ripped the tape from my mouth. Ouch, it hurt like hell...Black Bastard!

"This is how this works," The guy started. "You only get one call. 150,000 if they wanna see your black ass alive again. They got 24 hours to come with the cheddar...24 hours and not a second later. Real Talk...Understood."

Of course I understood but damn, how the hell was I supposed to come up with that much cash. Had they been ill informed? What did they think, that I had bundles of cash hidden away in a wall somewhere? For a second, Prina thought I was playing some type of cruel joke until she stopped for a moment to hear the tremble in my tone. This shit was real and I had a giant gash in my head to prove it. I told her to call whoever she thought could come up with the money. 24 hours…damn, I was a dead man. I could read the headlines now, "RISING SUN leader found dead, shot multiple times…Then they'd go on to sum up my whole life in one column. Maybe I'd become a Martyr in my death. They say, "**You're Nobody Until Somebody Kills You.**

Chapter

14

Prince sat alone in his modest home away from home in Suburban Ashbury Park New Jersey in deep thought. On the balcony where he sat relaxed, feet propped up, soaking in the remarkable ocean front view of the Eastern shore, he thought of how complex things were becoming back home. The struggle within his hometown had become an obsession and he was driven to conquer the city by any means. And lately with these recent murders, he felt he needed to remove himself from the scene for a minute...analyze and regroup. It seemed like the stronger he got, the higher he climbed up the success ladder, the more persistent the forces working against him got. Prince wasn't an average mediocre cat. At the present, he was a hundred million dollar boy and running. He was grinding hard and making all the right connections. And this Black Wall St. business was just the tip of the iceberg. The whole idea was larger than life. An idea that the Power Structure had fought for many years to undermine but Prince could now feel the forces at work, now more than ever which is why he had to fall back and gather his thoughts. Get away from it all and just relax and exhale...

The Boss, Ricky Ross, penetrated the air waves as Prince reclined back on his balcony, gazing out at life on the shore.

Porsche Cabrera Cazal shades covered his hazy eyes. He toked on a joint of Cush in between taking puffs from the Cohiba as the Maybache music took him back to the streets. There was still a lot of street in him, more than he wanted to admit. But he managed to suppress the wild streak, although at times it was a struggle. Clouds of Cohiba cigar smoke filled the air as the O.G. observed the tourist stroll along the beach. Children played joyfully near the water's edge and some built sand castles. Prince smiled fondly at the sight of them as Dawn, his 9 year old princess came to mind. He made a mental note to make her his first priority once his brief recess was over. Suddenly, the alarming sounds from his house phone echoed through the house, which momentarily broke Prince's concentration. But once he answered the call and acknowledged who was on the other end of the phone, he automatically slipped back into combat mode as Kihiem's voice assured him that relaxation time was over and that it was time to go home and get to work...

"Here we go," Prince muttered and hung up the phone. He began making preparations for a relaxing bath after he paged his personal stylist for her to come through and pack a few bags for tomorrow's flight back to Richmond.

He caught the earliest flight available and made it back home in time to catch Wanda whipping up a delicious breakfast. They had a long list of properties in the city, but where they felt most comfortable at whenever they were in town, was their newly built Condominium out on Short Pump Dr. It was nice and cozy and lavishly decorated with all the right accessories fit for a prince and his queen. He called from the airport informing Wanda of what time to expect him. It was approximately 6:25 in the morning when he arrived. The moment he hit the door step, he took a moment to savor in the pleasant aroma coming from inside.

'Now that's a real woman for you,' he was thinking as he approached the door. Wanda knew without having to be told, what to do for her man. Fifteen years of marriage and still, they were tight as hell, still incorporating new ways to please one another. Prince used his key to let himself in. Closing the door behind him, to his surprise as he turned around, there Wanda stood as lovely as she wanted to be in the middle of their living room. She held a platter filled with his favorite morning dish. Grilled Salmon, cheese eggs and hash brown with fresh fruits on the side….however as scrumptious as the meal looked to his eyes, it was Wanda's striking appearance that left him spell bind. Damn….even at 40, she was still a winner. She was stark-naked under the lavender sheer Camisole gown that length, stopped just below her shapely thighs. Her four inch heels complimented her height making her look a few inches taller. "I hope you're hungry baby," was how she greeted Prince as she stood there beaming.

"Come over here you," Prince replied giving her the come hither look. The see through garment left nothing to imagine. Her perky little tits were mouth watering and the nibbles on them were hard and pointed like missiles ready to discharge. She was well aware of how crazy and beastly that piece made Prince. He loved that damn gown. As she strutted off to put the food on the countertop, her perfect apple shaped ass shook with skilled precision as though she did it purposely. God she was beautiful. Her long cold black hair, she had separated into two girlish pony tails that draped pass her shoulders. Time had served her well. She was still that pretty little thang he'd bagged at Williamsburg Skate land over 20 years ago. Her cocoa brown skin tone was so smooth and radiant and sweet like a peach. Prince could almost taste her from just watching her. He let the luggage in his hand fall to the floor as he opened his arms to receive his gem. She melted in his comforting arms.

"So..."Wanda began, "Which would you like first, breakfast or would you like to skip it and go straight to dessert." She then guided both of his hands over her voluptuous hips as he sensually sunk his claws deep into her tender buns.

"Interesting" Prince said, "Because I've had this damn sweet tooth in my mouth all morning."

And suddenly, they were all over one another. The living room had become their little private freaky playhouse. Prince was a bedroom bully and like always, he gave his wife the business. From the velvet carpet, to the plush leather sofa and the countertop, the couple fucked like two wild sexually deprived indolence's in heat. On the countertop, Wanda wrapped herself around Prince's solid frame and commenced to pulling him deep inside her. And soon after, her body was rewarded with an overwhelming feeling of pure pleasure. Their kisses were passionate, their bodies intertwined as one. The love they shared for one another was more than evident. By 9:30, both of them were dog tired, tucked under silk sheets recuperating. Though he wanted to sleep, he couldn't because Kihiem and his wife, Pearl would be by at 11:30 to drop off Dawn. She had spent the weekend with their daughter Assata. But dropping off Dawn wasn't the only reason for Kihiem's visit. They had a lot to talk about.

For instants, Nat's inability to control his affairs (Fridays night's triple homicide)...When the murders had first occurred, Prince thought that from his discussion with Dip, that

maybe he'd went ahead and murdered the youngsters, thinking that it was what his boss had insinuated. Under that
impression, Prince took it upon himself to see Dip personally.
He just couldn't believe that Dip had done it when he'd
specifically told him not to. Prince scorned him but Dip
admitted that he had made a mistake, but murder wasn't it. In
following through on Prince's orders, that is, to go at the
brothers peacefully and convince them to take their dealings
out of the neighborhood, some of Nat's followers were
around. They over heard the discussion between Dip and the
three guys which turned into a heated dispute. And everyone
knew him to be somewhat of an enforcer for Prince. They
knew of his reputation as a gun slinger, but also, they were
aware of the transformation he had made in recent years. But
what they failed to realize is that, under the right circumstances and a real cause, he still had a quick temper and a itchy
trigger finger. But the murders were not his work. Of course,
Prince was more than relieved to hear that. The down side to it
though, was that lives had been lost in his territory. Already
the relentless media and newspapers were having a field day.
They were more concerned about tarnishing the organization's
good record than the lives lost. Then there was Nat Turner...the guys who had committed this terrible crime, were
supposedly potential followers of his. Dip explained that his
only mistake was confronting the men in front of Nat's followers.

    Black Wall St. was no secret society. Everyone knew
Prince and what he was trying to accomplish. And so when
these cats overheard Dip and the youngsters showing resistance, it's a good possibility that they felt it was their duty to
step in. Apparently, they thought they were doing Prince and

the establishment a solid by offing the cats...maybe. Dip left
the area for a few hours in an attempt to ease the tension and
hopefully come up with a better resolution. But when he
returned, he found a bloody mess. There was confusion, cops
and yellow tape blocking off the perimeter, the usual murder
scene. Straight up fuckin cowboys, talk about furious, Prince
was past that point. It took years to establish what Black Wall
St. had built in the community. The residents believed in the
Prince of Peace...The organization was the people's only
hope...and now this. Prince told Wanda that he needed to be
alone with Kihiem so when they finally arrived, she and Pearl
stayed long enough for Dawn to greet her father and then they
were right back out the door.

"Do you mind," Prince asked gesturing to the cigar in his
hand that he was about to flame.

"Yes, I do" Kihiem replied as he took a seat. Prince lit his
cigar anyway. Kihiem simply shook his head. He expected
nothing less from Prince. Several minutes of their talk was
centered on Nat's abduction and his recovery among other
things... There were some loose strings. Although Kihiem
couldn't quite put his finger on it, something in this milk just
didn't seem clean. It was one of those gut feelings. When the
call had first come in during the wee hours of the morning
from a panicked Prina about ransom money in exchange for
Nat's life, Kihiem's first instinct was to contact Prince. Who
the hell else could swing that amount of money in such a short
time? But Kihiem remembered his discussion with Prince the
next morning. He just thought his friend was extra cool...too
calm about so serious a situation. But then again, maybe he
acted in such a manner because it was no problem for him to
get the ransom. That made sense. Prince said that he'd take

care of it and shortly after, Nat was released...Just like that. He had this insane thought in his head about Nat's abduction and the people involved... It was too absurd to even share with anyone but the damn thing kept him up at night.

"Something you wanna talk about, "Prince said and crossed a leg over the other. "You've had this certain look on your face ever since you got here." A pull off his cigar, he looked straight at Kihiem, half smiling as he let go of a cloud of smoke. "If something is on your chest, now is the time to get it off."

At that point, Kihiem was convinced that his assumption had been correct. Prince was engaging him to act...to speak his mind so that the slate between them could be wiped clean. And so he said. "Brother," he finally spoke, drawing Prince's undivided attention.

"You're playing a very dangerous game... one that I definitely want no parts of Prince; the brother could've really been hurt, or even worse, killed!" Kihiem spoke with conviction in his voice and hurt in his eyes. "Help me understand your angle, Prince because right now, this move doesn't make sense to me"....

"Remember all those years back when we was just teenagers doing petty stick ups?" Prince hesitated waiting on confirmation from Kihiem. "Do you remember?"

"Yeah of course, but—

"Let me finish," Prince cut back in. He went on about a robbery where they had stuck a man up for some chump change and his sneakers. The guy had somehow run into a police car that he flag down a street over after Prince and Kihiem had ripped him off. The next thing they knew, they had a police chase on their hand. After blocks and blocks of hard running, Kihiem out of breath had literally given up. But Prince was so determined not to get caught and so he dragged his friend until they reached safety. Prince reminded him of a later time when Kihiem was being held at gun point and suddenly, Prince again came to his rescue. He shot a guy dead and then had to go away and do a four year prison sentence for it.

"What is this Prince? Do you wanna make me feel bad? Is that it? What the hell does any of that has to do with right now?"

"It has everything to do with it!" Prince barked back, the tone in his voice rising slightly. He resumed "As long as I can remember brother, I've been protecting you and saving your ass. Back then and even now, I'm still looking out for you...You just don't know it yet."

"Protecting me from what Prince and from whom...Nat?"

"I'm protecting you from your own destructive self brother."

"You trippin man" Kihiem replied. "How did we even get here? We were talking about Nat and you just took it left field on me."

"Can a devil fool a Muslim?" Prince asked suddenly.

"Not now day," Kihiem answered sincerely.

"Why do you have so much confidence in Nat.?"

"Because he's a good brother, I don't know...There's just something sincere about him. Shouldn't we support his movement? It's legitimate and its strong man. Am I missing something?"

"So you trust him, huh."

"Yes Prince; I would say that I do trust him."

"Well I don't so you keep that mutherfucka away from me..." Prince demanded. "I'm sorry man. Surely you can understand my passion. It's just that...we've worked too hard, I got too much money invested in this and to allow some sucker we don't even know to interrupt this flaw is not going to happen. I found out that some of Nat's people were behind those murders. That's our territory man. Black Wall St, the Prince of Peace....that's our shit. We built this from nothing! Everything we have man, we had to get it from the ruff..."

"So did you do it, Prince? You know what I mean."

Silence fell over the room for a spell then Prince drew in a long sigh and looks straight across at Kihiem nodding his head. "Yes I did it man. I sent the goon squad at him." He puffed his cigar a few times, watching the displeasure on his friends face.

Managing a smile, Kihiem said, "So you a gangsta now huh, Prince"

"I ain't saying all that."

"You don't have to say it, brother. It's yours actions...Your actions are a direct manifestation of your thoughts."

"I'm simply trying to protect my interest, brother, you don't know what it's like to be Prince, so don't judge."

And I'm not judging...but look at you in the Prada slippers, smoking on your cigar," Kihiem laughed. "You back on that gangsta type time. "You got that look."

"Get the fuck outta here, "Prince said as the both of them doubled over in laughter at Kihiem's comment.

"You wrong brother for stereotyping me that way, don't make me call my man Al Sharpton. You know I got the number on speed dial." Prince looked down at his slippers and at the cigar. "I can't believe you call me a gangsta."

"And I can't believe you did that to Nat"

"Brother, I don't believe half of the shit I do."

"I'm serious, Prince"

"And I'm not?"

"What the hell has gotten into you?"

"Kihiem look, you already know how I feel about this dude. This cat is funny money, I'm telling you. I don't regret what I did. I think he's in over his fuckin head and don't know what the hell he's doing. And another thing"…Prince said as an afterthought. "Nat ain't off the hook yet either. I hold him responsible for those murders."

"Okay, let me say this at least." Kihiem interjected. "However you feel about the brother, that's your business. But your tactics are irresponsible and reckless. This ain't the 80's brother…Excuse my language, but you are a fuckin' multi millionaire. What we have built…it's beautiful, but if you continue moving in this same course, you're only going to give our enemy the rope to hang us. Now I'm your brother, I love you but you already know where I stand. I'm a soldier for Islam Nation."

For almost a whole minute, Prince didn't utter a sound. Truth was similar to the bitter taste of cough syrup going down. In taking the doses in an orderly fashion, eventually the sickness would begin to subside. And with truth, the mention of it could be like a piercing sound to the ears, rough and offensive even…But if accepted, that truth could be like the sun reflecting its light back to a dead earth. Every word Kihiem spoke was the truth. Maybe Prince had overreacted with Nat. Of course he had. And maybe he was still living in the 80's, getting his gangsta on. Of course, he was. Casting a quick glance down at his expensive footwear and then at the expensive $20 a pop Cohiba, Prince smiled inside reflecting back over his partner calling him a gangsta. It often took for someone close to point out ones error for it to really set in. Kihiem was the one, the truth teller. But although he knew Kihiem was right, Prince damn sure wasn't about to tell him.

Chapter

15

His watch read 11:50 am, still ten minutes until the appointed time Nat was asked to arrive. Prince always ate here at Star and Crescent. He was a proud owner. Soft jazz tunes momentarily put his mind at ease as he nursed a hot cup of cappuccino while reading over today's Times Dispatch. Then just as he glanced up toward the entrance, Nat's solid frame was making its way through the opened doors. He had become a physical specimen in prison, clearly weighing somewhere around 190lbs, standing over 6'2" with muscles bulging through his linen shirt. The two men embraced, greeting one another in a brotherly fashion. Prince asked Nat if he desired anything to eat or drink. Nat declined...

"Hey Prince...man I just wanna say thanks for what you did. As we speak, I'm trying to reimburse you" –

"How's your head, "Prince said totally disregarding Nat's comment about the money he allegedly put up for him. He then added, "The money, we can discuss later."

"Cool", Nat said. "Well other than the 11 stitches, I'm good Prince, thanks for asking. Matter fact, a brother blessed to still be alive. For real, I'm just taking it in strides."

"I hear that."

"So what's up, your call sounded kind of urgent."

"It was urgent, Nat." Prince began with a locking stare into Nat's eyes and never blinked once. "Brother Nat, I'm sure you are familiar with my brother Kihiem's vision which is one that I faithfully share with him one hundred percent." Prince continued as Nat watched and listened attentively. "If you're not fully aware of our dedication to this movement, let me explain more. See Nat, in our city today, the **Powers That Be** would much rather continue to pimp the murder rate than to request more assistance from the Government while our brothers are dying in record numbers in the streets. As if our people weren't already struggling, the recession has choked the life out of them. They are walking around out here like zombies with no hope for a tomorrow, because it's a struggle to make it through today. But in light of all this Nat, the Black Wall St. establishment is trying to push through this depression. We gonna take it back to the early 1920's when we grew our own fruit and planted our own seeds, feel me?"

"Of course I feel you Prince" Nat replied. I'm with you man."

"The business is this," Prince went on. "Bodies, young bodies littering the soil that Allah, your God has blessed us to keep crime free for the past year..."Prince passed Nat the newspaper. "That is... until your coming."

Prince's last comment caught Nat by surprise. He looked stunned and speechless as they both shared a long stare. While Nat went on to read the full page article about the murders, which made the papers twice, Prince explained to him what had taken place that night.

"It ain't good, Nat. Not good for us and not good for the people who are dedicated to our movement."

Nat finished the article and was quiet for a moment con-templating...He rubbed his manicured goatee as he refocused across at Prince.

"So what do you need me to do Prince?" For a moment as Prince observed the extraordinary humility in Nat and to a degree, his conscious homed in on him. Here he was trying to bring unity amongst an entire community through the (P.O.P) Foundation and yet, he was searching for any reason possible to down play this brother's hard work. What the hell kind of hypocrisy was that.

Prince responded. "I'm glad you asked Nat. First I need you to pay for each of those kids burials out of your pocket. And secondly, if you are loyal to Black Wall St, Kihiem and I and most of all, Allah, I want you to reach out to the brothers responsible for this and make sure that something like this never happens again. And about the money I put up for you...forget about it."

"That's a lot of money, Prince. I gotta pay you back, I wouldn't feel right."

"Just worry about those brothers, okay. And handle the people up under you because they're your responsibility. This can never happen again, Nat."

'That was a lot of money', thought Nat. *"Don't worry about it."* He couldn't understand it, but what he did understand was the look in Prince's eyes as he spoke, which could in no way be misinterpreted. He was very serious. Prince then rose to his feet, patted the broad shoulder of Nat and whispered on his way out, "sit back down, eat, think, and pray brother Nat, I'll see you soon." Prince left Nat, walked toward the door of Star and Crescent's where David and Hot Rod were waiting. The three men exited the establishment without looking back.

Driving down Nine mile Rd, Prince received a call from his
lawyer Shabazz advising him of an invitation for dinner with
the city council and Housing Authority members. It was a
dinner date that Prince had long been anticipating.

Chapter

16

Nat Turner

I don't care if I never attend another funeral again in life. Neither of the young men who died was over the age of 25 years old. And just to think, it could've been me lying stiff in that pine box a week ago. The life I live...I didn't understand it. I wasn't in the streets no more, slanging poison and shooting pistols, yet the streets didn't seem to want to let be. At least I didn't have to pay the ransom money back. That was a good thing. I manage to scramble up half of it which was mostly proceeds from book sells. Prince wouldn't accept it. He didn't even want to discuss it. So I simply did as he had asked of me. I paid for all three of the funeral services. I was happy to do it. I'm guessing all this drama was all part of my trial. Failure wasn't an option. I was pushing on; RISING SUN had potential to be one of the strongest organizations around. I believe that Stanley Tookie Williams would be proud. RISING SUN was the fulfillment of his dream. To see the Bloods and Crips united at last. We were a long ways from it, but I was optimistic.

Meanwhile, I took Prince's advice and began to work strenuously on organization. We wanted to build human potential, not just recruit members for the sake of numbers which meant that I had to reinforce strict discipline and certain laws to ensure that what took place over a week ago, never happen again. Life is so precious and we need every soldier we can get. The future was looking bright. I just got the most exhilarating news. Before leaving the office, I received a call from The Ghost, the author of my autobiography. He was informing me that Random Publishing was interested in purchasing the rights to my book. To add, the book was also being considered for a movie. That's right; my life story would be portrayed on film. The Ghost wanted to know what I thought and would I consider agreeing to it. I mean, just what the hell he thought I'd say. I was so excited, that I ran through red lights trying to get home to my baby. I could've given her the good news over the phone but I wanted to do it in person. I wanted to see Prina's expression and share such a moment with her. Besides, it was because of her that we had been able to achieve the unthinkable. Plus, I had a very important question to ask her. I was about to make this thing official. In my pocket, was the most beautiful five carat Princess-cut diamond in Platinum. I was gonna ask Prina to be my wife. After of course, I gave her the good news. It was a perfect time as any.

Doug Jr. was there when I arrived, which was wonderful because I wanted him to hear it as well. "Guess what?" I blurted out the moment I walked through the door and found them sitting inside the living room den. "Yall not gonna believe this."

I had obviously interrupted something. I held my next statement as I noticed for the first time the look on Prina's face. I could tell that she'd been crying. Her eyes were red and puffy.

"Did something happen, what's going on?"

At that point, Doug Jr. rose up. "I'll leave so that you two can talk," he said all the while avoiding direct eye contact with me. 'What the hell was that about,' I wondered. I turned back to Prina who was still seated with her face cuffed in both hands. I heard the front door shut, a clear indication that Doug Jr. had left the house.

"Prina talk to me." I sat beside her on the chair and pulled her close into my arms, kissed her cheeks and looked deeply into her swollen red eyes and saw something alarming... For a moment, my heart trembled with fear from not knowing what had shaken her up. I was scared.

"Nat I can't do this anymore," She sprung to her feet in haste and began pacing.

"You can't do what Prina, What is this?"

"Oh my God..."She whispered and suddenly looked at me with this terrified expression that caused the hairs on the back of my neck to ruffle. "I've done something terrible. God Nat, I've been lying to you."

I watched her pace the floor like a nervous wreck. I had never seen her so upset before. What had she done that was terrible enough to send her over the edge like this? Did she not wanna be with me anymore? I felt for the diamond cluster inside my jacket pocket as I recounted her last words. "I've been lying to you..." She was seeing someone else...That had to be it. Son nova-bitch, I caught chest pains from just thinking about her and another man. How could she do this to me when I'd been so faithful? For the first time in my life, I was actually content with coming home to one woman. Past times must've caught up with me, Karma you Bitch! The very thought of Prina's betrayal ignited a fume within so great, that I snatched her by her arm and forced her down beside me.

"Sit your ass down and tell me what's going on!"

I made her confess, wished I hadn't because it was horrible. So much so, that after she was done telling me everything, I wished like hell that it had been another man. Indeed, she had been lying to me alright...from the very beginning.

It all began, so says Prina about six months before our first communication. At the time, she was living in DC working as one of the top journalist for the Washington Post newspaper, when she received a mysterious call from a guy who identified himself as F.B.I Agent Bryant Fisher. From that call, she soon learned that her son back home in Richmond, had gotten himself in a world of trouble. The Government had jammed him and a few of his friends up on drug related murder charges and already had sealed indictments with his name on it. Eventually she met with the Agents and was shown documents, witness statements in relation with Doug Jr's case. Her only son was about to go to prison for possibly the rest of his young life...unless. You know how the pigs do. They told her they could make it all go away if she played ball. Once Prina agreed, she was given a file on me and my potential rising organization which at that time, was just starting to get off the ground. Initially her objective was to one, get close to me and gain my trust; two assist me in my effort to build the organization up. It worked. She definitely had my trust from the start. She utilized her profession to gain recognition for RISING SUN by the numerous publications that she wrote. After fulfilling her obligation, prior to my release, she received one last request from her Agent friends. It was nothing major; in fact, it hardly would take any effort at all. They asked her upon my arrival to introduce me to the Black Wall St. family and upon the completion of that task; the charges against her son would disappear. And it was finished.

You can know someone your whole life and not really know them. I've never loved and respected a woman as much as I do Prina. She claims that in spite of the circumstances under which we met, that it was still not enough to stop her heart from wrapping around me. She said the stronger her love got for me, the more her secret began to choke the life out of her. That she had searched a many nights for courage and the right words to tell me. Now it was clear to me of why on many occasions, I would find her crying for no apparent reason. At night after making love, often times, I'd awaken during the wee hours of the morning and catch her pretty face staring at me through tearful eyes. A full year now, I've been sleeping next to this woman as though we were already husband and wife. This was the ultimate challenge for me, one that was a knock out. I had been sucker punched. I was physically weak, sitting there listening to my woman break me into little pieces. I know she loved me and didn't want me to leave but damn it, I had to go.

A relationship that was built on lies was a weak foundation. What part of her was real? She tricked me and the Government had humiliated me. I loved her so much that I hated her, if that made sense at all. Part of me was so ruined by what she'd done, that it took everything in me not to curse her and disrespect her, or even to put the big hand on her. I was mad enough to do it. But I was caught up in my emotions so I packed a few changing clothes in my favorite back pack but as I was heading for the door, Prina delivered another blow. It was knockout punch. Prina was pregnant. But even such joyful news wasn't enough to hold me there. I felt absolutely nothing, no compassion or sensitivity for her at that moment. I was numb. I jerked my arm away from her strong grip and slammed the door shut. I stormed to my truck, opened the passenger door and tossed my bag inside. Prina was in the door way as I rounded the truck about to hop in. I stopped and retrieved the black velvet box from my jacket pocket, opened it to gaze at the shinny diamond. Tear drops made my eyes burn as I cast one last glance at the ring then at the woman who was supposed to be my wife. I hurled the damn box with all the strength I could muster. I watched it disappear into the black night before I hopped in the truck and backed out of the drive way.

I found myself driving around in circles with no particular destination in mind. I ended up calling my partner, Dame down in Norfolk. We weren't on the line but a couple minutes and he could sense in my voice that something was wrong. He inquired but I shook it off and told him that I was simply stressed from work. I told him that I needed a break. And so Dame invited me down to Norfolk. I jumped straight on the highway. When I arrived there, Dame had set me up in the Presidential suite at the Sheraton Hotel. It wasn't until I got there, that I learned that he was throwing a party in the same hotel. It had to be at least 30 women coming from as far as Carolina and D.C. And Dame wanted me nowhere near his girls. He was still a bit salty at me for freeing Star from his stable. On a more serious note, though, he thanked me because he hadn't known of her situation. Out of all the dancers he hired to work for him, Star was one of the few who had appealed to him. Dame admitted that he was sincerely proud to hear that Star was advocating and addressing audiences all across the country about her condition. Dame and I talked about a lot that night, past and present. My mother, he said would be proud to see what had become of her young man. I wished that I could confide in my buddy about what was bothering me but I couldn't....It was something so complex that it was better not to talk about it..Not to anyone. I didn't wanna be around no one, especially women...not even topless dancers. Just me, myself and I, my pains and a bottle of get right. That's right...I relapsed. I took my first drank that night. I got gone off of that Patron. Man, I was in bad shape. But for the moment, I held the pain at bay...

Chapter

17

The excitement out on the Creighton Brook black top was similar to a historical Summer League event. From every crack and cranny of the slums, the finest players came out to compete for the 2500.00 dollar price reward. Ten teams, five men selected to a team with the winner receiving five hundred a piece, it was exciting to watch. Sponsored by Jacky Williams, representative of the alliance to conserve old Richmond neighborhoods, she and the (P.O.P) establishment was the brain child behind the Fundraiser designed to raise funds to cover expenses for their new free lunch program as well as remodeling the neighborhood rac center. But for the most part, it was all about bringing the community back together. Street cats with enormous talent from just about every part of the city, who under different circumstances, would probably be at each other's neck, came out for the peaceful event. Every month for the past six months, folks turned out in droves. It was a different place than in recent years with the presence of the (P.O.P) Foundation. The corners and cuts in between the project buildings were no longer occupied by dealers. Elders and children could be seen strolling the streets freely now because crime in the neighborhood had come to a halt. So outsiders felt comfortable coming out and supporting the fundraiser, indulging them-selves in the exquisite fun and entertainment. And there was never an incident which was partly due to the Islam Nation hosting the event. It always ran smooth. And with last month's guest appearance from Ben Wallace and his generous 10,000 dollar donation, the Fundraiser was quickly gaining popularity in the city and state.

The Cap City's number one D.J. Lonnie B mixed old school and new school ear friendly music, doing it big like the heavy hitter D.J. that he was. It seemed like every month drew a larger crowd. Today was straight up ridiculous. Vehicles hugged the streets, lined up from Punch Place to as far as Nine mile road. Without the participation of the neighborhood residents none of this would be possible. It was them who sweated over the smoking hot grills and assisted in organizing the whole event. Prina was among the gathering, she and her step-daughter Precious. She was Doug's older sister by their father's first wife. They were both there to watch his team compete for the prize money. It had been two years since the two women had spent time together. Precious now an Atlanta resident, along with her husband and their young daughter Ashley, between family life and her paralegal gig at one of the most prestigious law firms in Atlanta Georgia, there was hardly any time for family reunions. She'd definitely come along way. She wasn't particularly a fan of basketball and if it had been up to her, they'd be meeting over brunch. It was a reason for that. At the mere age of 13, she witness the brutal murder of her father right after a basketball game just like the one they were watching today. He was shot to smithereens right there in front of her on the black top. He took his last breath in her arms. It devastated her and for a long time she withdrew herself from the sport. The memories were just too painful. And even today as she observed her brother who bore a striking resemblance of their late father, run up and down the blacktop as her pops had once done, the images of that dreadful day was suddenly fresh in her mind. But it was so long ago. And she wasn't the little black girl lost anymore but a proud wife and mother with her own wonderful family. Indeed, Doug Carrington would be proud of his young woman.

It felt good to be back home and around her family for a change. Plus she'd been overly anxious to meet the mystery man in Prina's life, seeing as though everyone had nothing but nice things to say about him. She had told Prina that as soon as she could take leave from work, she'd do it, so that she could finally see the guy. But upon her arrival, she sensed tension. Prina wasn't her usual cheerful self and when she inquired about Nat, there wasn't any enthusiasm. Something had happened; she was sure of it. At the present, he was supposedly out of town on business, which meant that Precious would possibly have to return home without meeting him.

Life was a goddamn mystery. No matter what Prina did to try and put distance between her thoughts and the troubling mess she'd gotten herself into, it just wouldn't go away. Finally, the reality began to set in that she had really messed up bad. And even worse was the feeling that she had possibly lost her man. A million times she recounted in her head the foolish decision to confer and cooperate with that Agent. But if she hadn't, there's a good chance that she and Nat would never have met in the first place. And Doug would be gone from her forever. How the hell was she to foresee all this drama? She'd fallen head over heels in love with this man of whom FBI agents paired her with. They singled her out. And for what reason was she asked to make an impression on Nat....play the perfect caring journalist who'd help him launch a nationwide movement?

She wanted answers damn it and rebuked herself for not being the overly aggressive, inquisitive chick that got her career started. But she was only a journalist...a concerned mother. She knew nothing about the law. They took advantage, the intimidation bullies that they were. The FBI Agent scared the poor lady to death. The whole ordeal just confused her. She was told that her only concern should be with saving her son and to leave the rest up to them...meaning, don't ask questions. And that's exactly what she did. Her last and final assignment was to get Nat into the Black Wall St. circle, which was done effortlessly. Even now if she wanted to contact the Agent, it was no use because she couldn't. It was like the bastard never even existed...strange. Nat didn't buy it though...That she couldn't make contact. But she was telling the whole truth. She admitted that she had made a grave mistake. That she didn't understand what she was involved in. That she was in over her head and was sorry as hell because of it. Prina cried and pleaded for his forgiveness. "I can't change what I've done, Nat" she said, her brown face glistening with tears. She reached for his hand and pressed it against her tight belly.

"I'm carrying your baby and I love you...I really do." Prina expressed with all sincerity as she laid her head against Nat's broad shoulders.

"Hey," Precious whispers and nudges Prina's side playfully. "Are you alright," Precious asked concerned. From the moment she arrived in town, Prina hadn't been her normal self. And now catching her in a daze, she was certain that Prina was dealing with some personal issues. She'd never seen her so incredibly reserved.

"You can tell, huh." Prina finally spoke.

"Yeah girl, you've been tripping ever since I got here. I mean what's up, is something going on that we need to talk about?"

Prina took a deep breath and let go with a huge sigh. "Damn girl," is it that bad Precious probed.

With a forced smile, Prina turned to face her step-daughter who she thought was the prettiest thing she'd ever seen. God how she longed to break down and cry and just spill it all out but as much as she wanted and desperately needed to confide in a friend, it wasn't wise. For one, she didn't know how to explain in words what had happened. And second, she'd swore Nat to secrecy, not to discuss their business with anyone.

"Men problems girl...We had an argument, you know how it is. Nat spends more time on the road than he spends at home." It was half true.

"Is that it?" Precious shot her a skeptic look.

"Yeah, of course."

"Damn, you had me really worried." Precious giggled. "You had me thinking you had lost your best friend. Prina you tripping over nothing, at least you know he's handling his business and not out there running the streets."

"I guess you're right."

"You know I am. I mean, I haven't met him yet but from what I've heard, he's a good person. I read the book too." Precious smiled. "It's really good. Do you realize how many hoochies would love to be in your shoes? Now days you'd be lucky to find a half a man. You got more than that. He ain't a Doug Carrington, though," Precious added crediting her dad and causing Prina to blush like a child. Both of them shared laughter in the midst of all the pandemonium. It was if as though they were the only two people there on the bleachers. Prina marveled at how womanly Precious had become. It was just yesterday it seemed that Precious would take the two hour trip down to D.C to spend weekends with her. And now, she was giving her step mother men pointers.

"I'm glad you're here," Prina told her and gave her a huge sisterly hug...Suddenly before they could break their embrace, the deafening sounds of gun fire reverberated the atmosphere, igniting alarm throughout the crowds of people. The music stopped momentarily as necks turned and eyes darted around in search of the source of the disturbance.

"Are you alright?" Prina said alarmingly to Precious upon noticing how shaken she looked. She didn't answer right off, too busy absorbed in the relentless search for number 19 jersey. Once she spotted Doug Jr, she sighed in relief.

"My damn nerves are shot, Prina."

The disturbance didn't disrupt the event at all. But later, everyone would learn that the shots fired were in fact fatal. A block or so over from Punch Place, there was a Blue on Black crime. Unfortunately, it was nothing out of the ordinary for the Richmond community. Another young black adolescence executed by the hands of a cop. Justifiable homicide is how they'd rule as all the others...Just so happen, this time it was Little Corey...

Chapter

18

Nat Turner

I read a newspaper article this morning that pissed me the hell off. It was about The Ghost and him having to pull out of a scheduled appearance at a Bonds & Nobles in Houston, Texas where he was to do a book signing. Because of some cowardly, racist bigot, the brother had to back out and ultimately disappoint dedicated fans in the process. But it wasn't the first time that something like that had happened and in the author's words, it wouldn't be the last. I spoke with him briefly about the matter, simply expressing to him that I was concerned. He laughed it off and said that he couldn't even keep count of how many cruel messages and death threats he received on a regular basis throughout the week.

The racial tension around the country was indeed still a problem. Last week I had to fly out to Chicago and deal with a situation involving the new Chapter out there. While it was the funniest thing I'd ever heard or that could happen rather, yet at the same time, it was a very serious matter that needed to be dealt with. A few youngsters who'd recently joined on to the Chicago Chapter were riding one night through their neighborhood when they unexpectedly stumbled upon a mysterious, rust colored Ford pickup truck with Confederate Flag stickers posted in the back window. The location was the

Southside…on elementary school grounds in a predominately black neighborhood. Two rednecks were spotted by the RISING SUN soldier's, one keeping look out while the other hung a noose from a tree where children sometimes sat under and ate lunch at the picnic table.

I don't have to tell you what happened next. Those white boys who were just a couple of wild teenagers got their asses kicked into the middle of next week. In the back of their pick up, were over a dozen nooses, which meant that these sick minded teenagers were gonna have a long night ahead of them. Not likely, they picked the wrong night and most definitely, the wrong location. Bloodied and battered, the three brothers forced them over to the tree and up on the picnic table, their hands bound. A pair of nooses were slung over their heads and tied tight around their necks and they were left there to look like the two jack asses that they were. The police found them one hour later. Other than the beaten they took, there wasn't any serious harm done, except for the pathetic sight of them. Somehow, the brothers were picked up two days later and charged with bogus, felony assault charges. Can you believe that? Was there a crime for hanging nooses….on school grounds? The case received national attention and the civil rights community was all over it. Their argument was that to charge one and not the other, was a double standard. The head of the RISING SUN Chapter, Charlie Mack requested my presence, so I caught a flight there to hear what had happened and to address the organization. I had a lot on my plate.

Around the country, the RISING SUN membership was steadily climbing. But sadly, we were still losing too many young men. Little Corey's untimely demise broke my heart.

He dies just when he's finally made the decision to start living. He was on his way to attend the peaceful fundraiser event, when a police cruiser pulled the car they were driving over. There was probably no particular reason, other than (DWB) Driving While Black. No weapons, no drugs were found, yet the trigger happy, white police officer fired four shots into the car after the passenger bailed because of an outstanding warrant he had pending.

Little Corey died at the scene. I wept like I'd never wept before. This was a kid who was a product of his environment. He didn't wanna be in the streets. I was really starting to get through to him. The message of life was just beginning to sink in....Damn. These cops were going hard out here, killing us without conscious. I mean, they'd gone mad. It was the third incident in just six months where a young black male had been mowed down by their hands. They were like ferocious blood hounds tasting blood for the very first time and just couldn't get enough. Their days were numbered....

After a couple days away from home, I ended up going back to Prina. I drank myself silly that first night and the next morning, I was worse off. No one can whip you or torment you more vehemently than your own conscious...you know that self accusing spirit. I didn't realize I could slip that easily. As if my problems could be solved from drowning myself in self pity. It was all just an illusion anyway. Even Dame could clearly see that I was out of pocket. He stopped by the Hotel suite where I was staying, took one look at me, shook his head and said, "This ain't you no more, playboy. Whatever the hell it is that's got you all bent out of shape, you need to take your ass home and work it out."

There's no feeling like betrayal, particularly by someone who you hold in high regard. For Prina, I would give her my kidney or a lung if there was ever a need because that is how much I adore her. And in spite of the bombshell she dropped on me, nothing had changed. I had a lot of time to think about our situation and for me to pass judgment on her without clearly knowing the circumstances, wasn't wise. But what I do know is that, a house divided can't stand. Together we could figure this thing out. It wasn't a secret that the FBI was somewhere working behind the scenes trying to undermine and disrupt the movement. It's what they've always done throughout history to just about every black liberation movement. Why should it be different today? I felt it though…The pressure from on high. The stronger we got, the hotter it got. I was at war…at war with myself. The beast inside was getting harder and harder to contain. It was difficult to remain sane in the midst of insanity. Poverty, pain and death is what I saw on a daily basis. But what bothered me the most, is the lying politicians in Government, law enforcement and their aggression toward black folks. Weren't we already struggling enough and yet all they did was add salt to our opened wounds.

Maybe I needed anger management or something. The Ghost had an interesting analysis. In lectures that he would deliver to historical Black colleges, he would break down how his writing stimulated from anger and pain. And that instead of acting out on those weak emotions through physical violence, it was through his pen, that he began to unleash the destructive demons. Instead of drawing the blood of another brother, he made his pen bleed. He had a favorite quote that he ended every lecture with. "Your mind can be your friend, or your mind can be your enemy, it depends on how you use it."

I liked that. I had my own relief system though. When I started to entertain those weak emotions, it was to the gym. They had this 80 pound heavy bag there that I'd wail on for sometimes an hour straight. That bag was my foe. I hated its guts. I'd slug at it, delivering powerful head and body shots until there was nothing left inside me. No anger...no pain, just pure exhaustion. The next day after Little Corey was laid to rest, I was so damn mad, that I fractured my wrist from slugging it so hard. Well, it wasn't as constructive as The Ghost's concept but at least, I wasn't pounding on another brother.

Chapter

19

"He did what?" asked Kihiem as he rose up in his chair and leaned forward across his Oakwood desk in pure astonishment. The young lady, Tiffany Bullock and her older brother Harry had just hit him with some earth shaking news. A serious accusation that he wished like hell wasn't true. Tiffany hadn't stopped crying since she entered his office. And Harry was furious and had this treacherous look of a person whose sister had been violated. Kihiem understood his anger. It was a natural reaction. In just another ten years, Assata would be Tiffany's age and God forbid that something like that could ever happen to his baby girl. Some savage man forcing himself on her. There would be nothing to discuss. The act alone deserved nothing less than a death sentence. And there was no force strong enough that would keep him from serving swift justice. Unfortunately though, this particular incident was a bit more complex than expected. The accused wasn't a predator in the true sense of the word but an anointed man of God. Tiffany Bullock and her family had been long time members of Reverend Rodney Patterson's congregation. As a little girl growing up in the church, she marveled with delight at the handsome, well spoken Pastor. In her innocent eyes, he was perfect. But she grew fast, developing a full figure with physical attributes that would make any sane man do a double take.

Suddenly there was a different look in his eyes on Sunday's, so says Tiffany. She described how the Pastor began making passes at her when she'd perform volunteer work at the church and how his hugs and forehead kisses were just a tad bit more than friendly. Things had come to a head the night before. One of the last volunteers to leave the church that late evening, the Pastor called her up to his office. It was there in the Reverend's sanctuary that Tiffany claimed to have witnessed a different side of the respectful, well mannered preacher. He literally tried to take her right there in his office. From the look of things, the situation had really devastated this girl. It was no secret how immoral and despicable some of the sick and perverted things that went on in the name of God had become. Brother Minister knew all too well of the hypocrisy that went on behind the pulpit. Every religious community had their faults and the Reverend was no exception. But rape? It was a hard pill to swallow. Kihiem and the Pastor had been friends as well as business partners for years. He was a major asset to the success of the Black Wall St. establishment. They'd all been working together to better the city's ravished neighborhoods. This was bad for everyone. He wished Nat was here to deal with this, being that Tiffany and Harry hadn't too long ago joined his organization. This was his business...or was it?

The youth of the community was every ones business; at least it was supposed to be that way. That concept was the whole dynamic principle in which the (P.O.P) Foundation was built upon. He'd already made the decision in his mind as he sat there with Tiffany, that he would go and pay the Pastor a personal visit. But with caution because the wrong approach could cause a rippling effect, still someone had to address the Reverend and obviously that someone just so happened to be Kihiem. It was better if he went instead of law enforcement or even worse, the media. The girl and her brother left him with a lot to ponder over. He hated being in such a comprising position, the Pastor was beloved by so many. He had done so much good, given so much of himself to the Richmond Community. Kihiem's main concern was simply to do the right thing. So if that meant going to speak to him personally about the matter then he was prepared to do so. Obviously, she felt desperate to come to Kihiem for help. Unless she just felt that she could trust Brother Minister. And she felt right. This type of nonsense was so prevalent in the community and in many cases, the incidents went unattended. But this time, it had landed in Kihiem's back yard. His heart and conscious wouldn't allow him to sit still and keep quiet about it. He made some phone calls and found out that the Pastor was working late at the church. Kihiem got him on the line and said that if it was alright, he wanted to stop by. Pastor told him that he was just finishing up and was about leave, but said that if he could get there in the next fifth teen minutes, he'd wait. The Youth Center being on the same side of town as the Pastor's church, Kihiem was there in less than ten minutes. The choir was inside rehearsing. He could hear them getting busy as he approached the beautiful structure. There was nothing like some good old gospel music and the choir singing was out of sight. Kihiem greeted the chorus as he entered and they all responded simultaneously.

The Muslim and Christian community had never been tighter than they were at the present, thanks to Brother Minister. He worked hard to establish the bond that they now had. Kihiem was so determined to unite with his Christians brothers, that shortly after his release from prison; he would just pop up at a Sunday morning service alone and grab a seat amongst the congregation. Soon after, he was introduced to Pastor Rodney Patterson. Kihiem being a Muslim and all drew curiosity from some of the church goers and even the Pastor himself. They wondered what the hell business a Muslim had in a Christian church. Kihiem simply told them once from the podium where he received an invitation to speak to pastor's congregation, that he loved the word of God, whether it came from the mouth of a Christian or Muslim. From that lecture, a very special relationship was born. It wasn't too long afterwards, that Pastor Rodney was brought in as a team player and ultimately becoming a senior investor in Black Wall St.

"I see you made it." Pastor Rodney said as he glanced up from his paperwork and found Kihiem standing there at his door. "Well come on in and have a seat brother. I'm just finishing up here." He was still scribbling something down as Kihiem made his way over and sat in the empty chair across from him. Often times what a person feels inside, can often manifest and show in a person's expression or demeanor. From the moment Kihiem had stepped foot inside the office, the Pastor had sensed an ill spirit, which was highly unusual for his Muslim brother. In all his years of dealing with the I.N, their positive attitude and warm smile was what stood out but today was a different story. The smile seemed to be void of substance. Kihiem didn't intend for it to be that way. He was so occupied in his thoughts with trying to make his presentation as less offensive as possible that it hadn't dawned on him that his wounded spirit had began to seep out through his pores. Preacher man observed Kihiem once more before finally placing his ink pen down gently on his desk. He leaned back in his comfortable swivel chair, retrieved his wire frame reading glasses from his tired eyes then asked. "You look a little tense brother, is everything alright?"

"Honestly Pastor, I'm not." Kihiem sighed deep and hard and shifted nervously in his seat. "I got some heavy stuff on my heart that I need to lay on you."

"Really,"...Preacher man uttered while studying Kihiem carefully. He'd never ever seen Brother Minister so apprehensive and at a loss for words. Obviously, this was a serious matter.

"Whatever I can do to help, brother," Preacher man said. "Just tell me what's happened."

"It's not about me Pastor," Kihiem told him still trying to choose his words carefully. Brother Minister paused to allow his words to resonate while he examined Preacher mans reaction, hoping to detect in it some sort of sign of foul play. But there was nothing there. He continued on. "I got a visit today from a member of your congregation."

"My congregation" Preacher man's brow rose in surprise.

"That's right." A short silence, then Kihiem finally loosened the knot in his tongue. There was no easy way to say it, so he simply gave Preacher man the whole spill on the young lady, Tiffany Bullock. He told the Pastor about their conversation, the accusations, the whole nine.

"You gotta be kidding me." Preacher man responded in a wave of shock. Kihiem didn't speak. "My God...you mean to tell me that you'd believe such nonsense."

"No brother, I wanted to come to you personally. I'm only here to find out the truth."

"The hell you are." Preacher man snaps back. His breaths were heavy and his tone much harsher. "Where is she?"

"She's scared Pastor. She wouldn't come."

"This doesn't make any sense at all. Its nonsense...I'm the most consistent preacher in the city. I've done nothing but good for that family. I don't believe it." Preacher man was up out of his seat pacing the floor. Then he stopped, turned towards Kihiem with a sadness in his eyes that made Brother Minister shudder.

"All over the country, we hear about sick Catholic preachers molesting little children...so called men of God taking advantage of innocent kids..."Preacher man never took his eye away from Kihiem. "They give men like me a bad rap. I'm a true man of God who strives in righteousness. I'm one of the few Christian preacher's around that preach the true gospel of Jesus Christ...You said you came to find out the truth...Did I try to rape that child," Preacher man forced a painful smile to his lips. "Brother you break my heart."

"It's not what you think, Pastor. You think this was easy for me to come here and do this. If the shoe were on the other foot, I'd expect you to do the same... Brother you know how I feel about our children."

"That young lady used you brother. For what, I have not the slightest idea. But she lied to you and you believed her."

"You're wrong Pastor."

"Your eyes said it all brother Kihiem. You looked at me as though I was dirty...foul." Preacher man shook his head. He took a deep breath then exhaled slowly. "At this time brother, I would really appreciate it if you'd leave."

"I'm sorry, Pastor if I offended you."

"Now man, just leave!" Preacher man was angry at Ki-hiem, unveiling a menacing side of himself that Brother Minister had never before seen. It shocked the hell out of him and for one split second as he observed the brewing rage in his eyes, the crease forming in his wrinkled fore head, he wondered if possibly that same formidable side of him, was what frightened Tiffany Bullock. There was no real proof other than the petrified girl herself. Could the Pastor have been right about Kihiem? Had his compassion for women over shadowed his ability to reason? Did he treat Preacher man too harshly? To stay and try to reason with him would only make matters worse.

Brother Minister had this very awkward feeling leaving Preacher man's office. Like maybe he had made a real bad mistake. Like maybe his actions had compromised future business plans with their up and coming Black Wall St. ventures. He should've definitely given it more thought before confronting him. Then there was Prince. He would most certainly be disappointed with this. He should've consulted with Prince first. Nevertheless, it was done and there was nothing else to do now but deal with the repercussions...Whatever the hell that was...

Chapter

20

It was his birthday weekend. A couple days of pure relaxation would do Prince just fine. There was no place in the world like Black Mecca. For some reason, whenever Prince returned home to his Atlanta estate, the weight of the world seemed to lift from his broad shoulders. If he so desired, he could hop in his fully loaded 62 model Maybache and not feel out of place. A-Town was home to a surge of celebrities and every where he looked, flashy, luxurious whips cruised the streets. Like for instance, Prince's first day back in town, he rubbed shoulders with his old friend Shawn Combs... (P. Diddy). While he waited patiently for a red light to turn at Lenox Rd, an almost identical Maybache drove up on his right.

It was two tone black and Chocó with the black leather interior, reclining rear seats. Almost simultaneously, both curtains rolled back and each occupant regarded one another in admiration and respect. Then the light changed. Not too long afterwards, he met back up with the Superstar at his restaurant. Prince loved to be around other successful people, particularly those who were worth as much as Shawn Combs. It kept him humble and hungry and constantly on the grind. After splurging the town, he had Hot Rod and David to drive him home. His wife was there waiting for his arrival. Around

nine o: clock he drove up to 10, 000 square ft of pure elegance.
A brick mansion nestled away on a ten acre wooded lot of
Georgia pines. A million and a half was a steal for the eight
bedrooms, four and a half bathrooms with a gas log fireplace.
A paved drive way leads directly to the main entrance, as well
as a huge six car garage. Once inside the modest home, it was
clear to see that it was suitable for a prince. He had a mini
theater installed with a 100" inch projection screen and a
personal gym.

Sliding doors gave way to a patio that was attached to a
heated in ground pool with a swim up bar. It was a helluva
place. Inside the house, he found Wanda and Stacy relaxing in
front of the enormous big screen while they nursed a couple
glasses of Bacardi lime. Sex & the City had the two of them
cracking up. The theater was most definitely his favorite place
in the mansion. The whole lay out was magnificent. A circular
leather sofa with enough room to seat at least ten people
wrapped around the spacious room and on both ends, set
accommodating matching foot rest. Directly in the center of
the sofa, was a marble table with over head lightening.

"How ya'll lady's doing?" Prince acknowledges the wom-
en upon entering the room. He walked straight over to Wanda
and landed a soft one dead on her sweet lips. She then gave a
quick introduction. "Honey this is Stacy Anderson."

Wanda had given Prince a heads up that she wouldn't be
home alone. Stacy was a potential customer who she met
through a mutual friend. She had an interest in some property
they owned down in Virginia. Born to a Dominican mother
and a Jamaican pops, she was currently residing in South
Carolina but desired to make a transition further up North to
be closer to her parents. Plus, she'd just ended a five year

marriage. She planned to sleep over and in the morning, they would take the long drive to Virginia to view the three bed-room tri level home. After everyone got acquainted, Prince found himself trying to avoid direct eye contact with Wanda's company. He didn't want to look at the strange woman too long. On a scale from one to ten, she was a 20, absolutely stunning. Buttery pecan tan complexion that was smooth as a baby's ass and her naturally cold black hair toppled down pass her shoulders. Even in her conservative attire; one could easily tell that she'd taken on her African American genes. The two piece business suit did nothing to hide the treasure underneath. Honey was fine as hell. Prince fixed himself a couple straight shots of Grey Goose and downed them right there at the bar. He lit up a cigar, poured another drink and joined Wanda on the sofa.

'What the hell did people see in this shit?' Prince won-dered about Sex & the City. Three old unattractive white women that wore entirely too much make up, he laughed inside at how consumed Wanda seemed to be in the movie. A few minutes of sitting there, Prince began to feel the liquor having an effect on him. And in that same instant a weird and almost ridiculous feeling suddenly had come over him. He felt this crazy energy coming from Stacy. He thought that she was staring at him. For a while he avoided even looking her way but he felt a pair of eyes clocking him hard. So finally, he let his gaze fall over in her direction. This was exactly the reason why he'd tried to avoid her. Her alluring eyes were like a bottle of sweet wine. One sip of it, you just had to have anoth-er taste. She had been indeed staring at him and now, Prince found it difficult to ignore her strong presence. Damn what a dangerous game to play with his woman sitting so close by.

Things got more intense with each passing second…the room seemed to have gotten warmer.

'It had to be the straight shot of Goose,' he thought. Honey didn't just lick those sexy full lips and seductively bite down on the bottom of it. Was this chick serious or what? Did she not know that Wanda was half crazy and would stomp a mud hole in her pretty behind if she even thought that she'd been disrespected in her own home. Prince shot a nervous glance at Wanda but luckily, her eyes were locked on the TV screen. Stacy kept at it. She couldn't stop moving. She rubbed her hands between her steamy thighs and over her nice firm tits. The mere sight of her carrying on that way aroused him. The bulge poking out from his sweat pants brought a look of comfort to her face. This was so not right, just what the hell did he think he was doing. 'Get your ass up right now and leave,' warned the voice in his head. He heard it loud and clear, yet this had never happened to him before. Any minute now Wanda would catch on and all hell would break loose. Then suddenly, Stacy got up and excused herself to the restroom. Boy was he relieved. The room was silent for a few minutes. Prince was pondering over whether or not he should address Wanda about the situation. Just when he'd got up enough nerve to give her the spill on her freaky friend, she sprung to her feet in a hurry.

"I wanna drink, you want one," she said and scurried off toward the bar. No sooner had she darted off, a minute or so later, Stacy reappeared. And what an appearance she made. Her hair had been swept up and tied in a neat little pony tail. The conservative apparels had been tossed aside and now she stood there in nothing but a tasty sheer negligee and some very tall 6 inch stilettos heels. There was not a flaw on this woman. Her hour glass figure was saturated in baby oil. Prince sat stunned, unable to utter one syllable. Over his shoulder, he glanced back at Wanda who stood at a safe distance.... watching him. She was beaming...who would've ever thought...She was such a naughty girl. All of a sudden, the room around him began to spin in circles. Stacy was in front of him now, her hips swaying side to side, seductively and engagingly. This had to have been staged because from out of nowhere, music began to leak from the speakers while she danced and fondled her self before him. He could feel his nature rising as she descended down to her knees in front of him and commenced to gently caress him. Then she took him out and boldly wrapped her luscious lips around his hardness and began slow necking him in a way that made every hair on his neck stand.

"Happy early birthday, baby," he heard Wanda's soft whisper from over his shoulder. She said that and met his lips with a sensational kiss. Then another and another until their lips were locked in an animalistic squeeze.

One must be careful what they ask for. For years now, Prince would tease and probe his wife about bringing another female into their bedroom. And like most women, Wanda always shunned the idea; in fact, it wasn't even up for discussion. Of course, Prince was only joking. In the past, he'd do the threesome thing in a minute but not with his wife. Hell no, other chicks were a different story. They were fair game. Obviously, Wanda had taken his jokes to heart. For him to keep mentioning it there had to be some truth to it. It wasn't an easy decision to make. Sharing her goods with some strange undeserving chick was once not an option. It took years to muster up the courage to even consider it but reality

was, she married a player, not to mention a player whose
worth was millions. The way she saw it was, when and if he
got the urge for something different, why go out when they
both could share in the experience.

It was an awkward feeling for Prince. Being intimate with
another woman in front of Wanda, he didn't think he could
ever get use to it. But Wanda encouraged him to have fun and
not hold back. She told him that she only did it because she
loved him. And that there was nothing she wouldn't do to
please him...Damn...In his immature way of thinking, Prince
never even considered something like this with Wanda. He
felt that he'd look at her differently afterwards, as well as
possibly disrupt their tight bond. But it was totally the opposite. He actually felt closer to her. To do what she'd done for
him was not only bold, but it was a reassurance that she did
indeed love him.

Early the next morning, he awakened to find several messages on his Blackberry. Majority of the texts were from
Kihiem and it seemed urgent. He returned a few calls and
caught Kihiem at home. He was certainly not pleased with the
news from his brother. Kihiem expressed his regret about the
way he handled the situation with the Pastor. He admitted
that his actions were purely motivated out of emotion and not
intelligence. Prince told him to let him take care of the Pastor.
So much for relaxation, this was too serious and needed his
immediate attention. The Black Wall St. establishment was so
close to closing in on the biggest deal yet. A project which
consisted of the demolition of a total of ten blocks of Public
Housing projects in two different areas of the city. And
remodeling those chosen areas with approximately twenty
five homes for low income residents to be chosen by a black

community activist who supported families of violent crime victims. No less than an hour after his conversation with Kihiem, he was making preparations to fly back to Virginia. Wanda was mad as hell but nevertheless, she understood the importance of why he had to make the personal visit. But still damn it, this was her time. Prince assured her that he wouldn't be long. He just wanted to sit down with Preacher man and iron this thing out with him and Brother Minister. Nothing or no one was bigger than the idea of Black Wall St. He needed to be sure that Preacher man understood that very important fact.

At 12:30 noon time, Wanda drove him to the airport to catch his one o'clock flight. By his side, David and Hot Rod boarded the plane with him.

Listening to slow jams on his I-Pod, images of last night's wild sex escapade played back in Princes head like a DVD on repeat. His wife…damn, she was simply magnificent. And Stacy was out of sight. The two of them together were just amazing. They went at it for nearly three hours straight. He was so hung over that next morning, that he didn't see Stacy when she left. She was so lovely, a face that he'd never forget. Prince knew nothing about her or where she'd come from which was obviously the way his wife had wanted it to be. He couldn't help from smiling inside thinking of how Wanda had set the whole thing up. 'That was pretty slick,' he thought. She made it perfectly clear, though that what happened was only to be done on special occasions. Prince had a strong urge to do something really nice for his wife. She had plenty of diamonds and Chin Chiller furs and last year for her 42nd birth date, he purchased for her a brand new Maserati right off the show room floor. A trip would be nice. A place where the sky is always blue and the people's complexion are like skittles. She'd like that for sure. That was exactly what he planned to do, as soon as he was finish with the business at hand. It was thirty minutes until the plane was to land. Right then, he received a text message from his Attorney Shabazz. Before leaving Atlanta, Prince had instructed his lawyer to contact Preacher man and set up a private meeting for them to sit down when he got to town. Obviously, if Shabazz was texting him, it meant that he'd found Pastor Rodney. Prince hurriedly got him on the line.

"Yeah, it's Prince. I got your message." The plane should be landing in the next 30."

"Brother, I have some bad news", Shabazz expressed solemnly... "I found Pastor Rodney."

"Sounds like good news to me, brother. That's what I ask you to do, just tell me when and where."

"Prince, I'm at the MCV Emergency Center right now with the Pastor's family."

"At the Emergency Center" Prince uttered confused. "I don't understand, what happened."

"He's been hurt bad man. And it's not looking good Prince. I mean, he might die."

Prince could hear the emotion in Shabazz last statement. As he listened to the Attorney describe the terrible accident, he began to perspire. He could hear his heart beating in his ears. It was as if all the air pressure had been let out of the room. The collar of his shirt suddenly seemed too tight. He couldn't believe it. Preacher man had been a friend of his for years. Who in the hell would do such a thing?"

On one of Preacher man's late nights at the office, someone had tried to run him over while he was approaching his car

about to get in. The vehicle slammed into him literally crush-
ing him against his own car. An impact so powerful, that the
contact almost obliterated the man on sight. The collision left
him with a severe head concussion, a punctured lung, broken
rib cages, arms and legs broken...a cracked spine and lastly an
internal bleeding. He was lucky to still be alive. Prince hung
up with the attorney with tears burning his eyes. He called his
wife and told her to catch the next flight home. Preacher man
and his family needed all the support they could get...

Chapter

21

A convoy of SUV's was there at the Richmond Airport waiting for Prince when his plane touched land. Initially, the plan was to head straight over to the Emergency Center to be with the Preacher's family but at the last minute came a deeply mind boggling message from Brother Kihiem Muhammad. The text had an urgent over tone. Kihiem said he needed to talk to him immediately but not over the phone. Prince didn't even bother to call, he instructed the driver to get him to Brother Ministers home ASAP! Something stunk to high heaven. This uneasy feeling suddenly sprung forth. It was there stuck right in the pit of his gut. Could shit get any worse? Kihiem's damn message had him all messed up, his thoughts diffusing in a million directions. Prince felt like they were revisiting a page out of their grim past, a past that both of them had tried to put as much distance between as they possibly could. And to add to his paranoia, was the extra surveillance that had been on him from the moment he left the Airport. In addition to the unmarked department issued vehicles that normally followed him every freaking where he went, today for some bizarre reason there above his convoy, was a Spy Plane. It was identical to the one that had run out of gas while surveying the cat Robert Deniro in the movie Casino. Prince spotted the damn thing airborne the minute he stepped foot off the plane. And less than two minutes away from Kihiem's place, it was still there...But upon observing the pandemonium and busy activity as the convoy bent the corner of the street where Brother Minister, his wife and young daughter shared a home, it became unmistakably clear of the reason for the extra heat.

Just because you're paranoid, doesn't mean that there's no one following you. Nothing in the world could've prepared Prince for the spectacle in process. Police enforcement had blocked off the entire perimeter surrounding Kihiem's home. The Alphabet Boys were in place, as well as a news truck. It was a real clown show. The first thing that caught Princes attention as he hopped out of the truck was Brother Minister's F-150 pickup truck, strung up on a tow truck. A couple officers were escorting Kihiem away from the house in hand handcuffs. He saw Prince rushing up, David, Hot Rod and other (P.O.P) affiliates on his heels.

"I'm being set up!" Brother Kihiem yelled at his partner as law men pushed him into captivity. They slammed the wagon door shut. Attorney Shabazz was right there instructing Brother Minister to not open his mouth to the police. Pearl remained on her porch trying to shelter their daughter from seeing her daddy in such a manner. When Prince reached Pearl who was emotionally wretched, she kept reiterating Kihiem's words.

"Somebody's setting my husband up. They've done it," she cried.

Then it finally dawned on him. Prince drowned out Pearl's voice for just a second as he refocused on Kihiem's truck for the first time. From the angle he now stood, he could see what he wasn't able to see when he first drove up. The complete right side of the F-150s front end had been smashed. When the implication of what the damage done to that truck actually began to register to Prince, he was absolutely stunned. It couldn't be…It just couldn't. For a short spell, his mind totally blanked. Pearl was talking, but he missed every word. Preacher man was almost annihilated by some crazed fool driving an unknown vehicle…At least that's what the news reported. But the vehicle wasn't unknown anymore. An F-150 fitted the bill perfectly. It possessed enough horse power to literally crush a person, as had been done with Preacher man. And from the looks of Kihiem's truck, it had definitely smashed into something…..a person maybe? In spite of how it looked, Pearl was more than convinced that someone else had done this. Attorney Shabazz followed the wagon and fleet of law enforcement down to the station while Prince sat with Pearl trying to make sense of it all. He tried to recount back in his mind the discussion he and Brother Minister had over the phone this morning before he left Atlanta. He couldn't detect in Kihiem's tone that he'd done something as hideous as this. Smashing a man of God to death with his pick-up truck, it was preposterous. He knew his brother, Kihiem wasn't capable of murder. Not at this point in his life anyway. But damn…the evidence though. They had the most important piece of evidence…his truck.

Prince thought…what if…what if he and Preacher man's meeting escalated into an exchange of dirty insults, a verbal altercation and possibly even physical. What if Preacher man was an undercover pervert that preyed on young girls? Brother Minister with his overly sensitive side when it involved women, lost the good sense that God had given him and sort to take care of the sick minded Pastor himself. Cut his ass down so that he'd never get a second try at fixing his greasy paws on somebody else's child. Wait a minute...just what the hell was Prince thinking? For God sakes, this was Kihiem here...Justice. A brother and true lifelong friend, no way could he have done this, he finally admitted to himself. But if he didn't then damn it, who in the hell did? That was the million dollar question.

It wasn't until later that evening; that things began to crystallize for Prince about this whole situation involving Kihiem. He was watching the breaking news with Wanda at their Condo. The media machine didn't waste any time in spewing out their propaganda. They made little mention of the brother's outstanding community work for the past several years. The anchor went straight to the meat and potatoes. They put close up pictures of Kihiem's battered F-150 and highlighted where they found what appeared to be traces of the victims blood there on the hood of the passenger side. Fragments of the truck were also found at the scene exactly where the vehicles had collided. Witnesses were materializing out of the woodworks. One eye witness saw the truck speeding away from the crime scene. Another claimed to have been present at the church the night Brother Minister had visited. The reporter said that there had been an argument between the two but as of yet, it wasn't clear what the cause behind the dispute was about.

And just when Prince thought it couldn't get any worse...it did. They dug up the worse picture of Kihiem they could possibly find. It was a 20 year old mug shot of Justice...the gangsta. To support the charge, reporters brought his past back to life, **The Notorious Juice Crew**... unsolved murders, Kihiem's federal conviction where millions in cash had been confiscated, along with a considerable amount of dope and properties. "Some people are just prone to violence...You can take the person out of the ghetto, but you can't take the ghetto out of the person...."

That was just some of the many comments from harsh critics. 'The nerve of those bastards,' Prince thought. These greedy vouchers were picking Brother Minister apart as though he was a dead carcass. What put the icing on the cake was seeing Preacher man's wife and family on the news. Prince did everything he could to prepare them for the media's slaughter. It was difficult to come to Kihiem's defense when the evidence against him was so overwhelming.

"I'm being set up, brother," was Kihiem's words.

"My husband is being set up...they've finally done it."...

"Set up by whom?" Prince couldn't help from thinking. Who would stand to benefit from the demise of the **Black Wall St. Enterprise?** Better yet, who were the beneficiaries of the total extermination of the historical Black Wall St. Originators? The bombing of an entire goddamned town filled with some of the most brilliant black minds to ever be produced from a people. Prince thought long and hard about his life. And the Government and how persistent they were when trying to attain a goal. They didn't expect for Prince to make it this far. And just as it was in the early days of them trying to pin bogus charges on him, so it was today. He'd beat every odd, defeated just about every obstacle and made his adversaries eat shit and taste his dust. Success was the best method for revenge... Prince's motto, even still, there was a price to pay for the idea in his head. Disunity and ignorance worked hand in hand. And as it had always been, a divided and ignorant people could easily be controlled and exploited. But

Black Wall St. was a threat to that opposing force. The Prince of Peace Foundation was attempting to unify and bring awareness to an entire community. Surely there were hidden powers working to under mind the organizations effort. But damn, Prince wondered, 'Could that same demonic mindset that bombed Oklahoma's Originators still be alive today? Could history be repeating itself? Had a poisonous virus seeped its way into their circle? Prince believed so. Something Funky was indeed in the air. He could smell a Judas....

Chapter

22

Nat Turner

I was having a son! I can't adequately describe the feeling but it was good...I guess joy and pain...sunshine and rain. While Prina and I were basking in joy, watching and listening to the sound of the baby's heart beat at the doctor's office, Pastor Rodney Patterson had died suddenly from complications at M.C.Vs Emergency Center. Everyone had been playing the waiting game. He was in such bad shape that not too many people expected him to pull through. But still we hoped he would. It was definitely a sad day, a time of great mourning for an entire community. Not even a week after the Pastor's accident and signs of aggression was already being seen in the people. The two communities Christian and Muslim were at odds. It was bad. Many of the Pastor's supporters wanted to penalize members of the Islam Nation because of the charges against Brother Kihiem. The tension had gotten so high that authorities intervened for fear of a civil war breaking out between the two groups. So there was around the clock squad cars' patrolling the area Mosque. Because of the friendship Brother Kihiem and I have, I was a bit leery myself of retaliation, so I beefed up my security. It was that real. But it broke my heart to see things change so dramatically. Brother Minister's bond was revoked. The judge had considered it but once the Pastor died, everything changed. His vehicular manslaughter charge was now murder one with criminal intent. So until his next court appearance, he would have to remain in protective custody down at the city jail.

I visited with my brother...I looked into that man's eyes and there's nothing no one can say to convince me that he did what his charges indicate. I don't care about the so called overwhelming evidence against him, Brother Kihiem didn't kill anybody! Prina shared my feelings. We knew about the dispute between the two men concerning the young lady Tiffany Bullock. But what the hell did it matter now. If Pastor did or didn't touch that girl, he was gone now. Our energy needed to be exerted toward fighting this case. The story made national headlines, clearly an indication of how powerful the media machine was. They were doing an excellent job in trying to slander the Islam Nation's positive image.

Headlines read **"Ex-criminal Turned Muslim Murders Reverend."** Then right along side of the article was Kihiem' face, it was a terrible picture of him. It was the old him. But he had a strong support system. Muslims from all over the country had come to his defense. And Prince had taken care of all legal matters. He hired a team of top notch lawyers to come in from as far as New York to assist Attorney Shabazz in this highly sensitive case.

Meanwhile with all this going down, I was making plans to sign off on a deal that would transform my story into film. The company had already bought the rights to the book. Aside from Kihiem's situation, things couldn't be better for me. The organization was thriving, memberships steadily growing. Atlanta and Baltimore were next on the list to establish Chapters. We were all over the place. Sometime during the month, I'd travel to those two states to speak with potential representatives. At home, Prina and I seemed to making head way. The new life in her belly was certainly one reason. I felt closer to her in spite of the circumstances. She was a good woman...my woman. I had yet to ask her to be my wife. She knew nothing about the 5 karat ring I had for her and I'm still kicking myself in the behind for throwing away that ring as though I could really afford it. Man what the hell could I have thinking? She'd make a good wife for somebody one day. I just didn't think that someone was me, but who knows what the future has in store

Chapter

23

Nat Turner
Morning of Pastor's Funeral

I didn't sleep at all last night. This day I'd been dreading all week. The reverend was our friend and we wanted to be there to mourn with everyone else. We should be there, yet we were outcast. We weren't welcomed. The Black Wall St. family had every right to be there. Prince and his wife and Kihiem's wife Pearl all wanted to attend the funeral but how would that look? Personally, I'd feel uncomfortable in such a setting, but I'd feel even worse if I didn't go. Prince brought up an interesting point when we spoke briefly over the phone earlier this week. He said it struck him as odd to see the F.B.I there at Kihiem's home when he was arrested. It was a state case and didn't warrant the FBI's presence. It didn't make sense to me either. But it did....

I could hear and smell Prina putting it down something serious in the kitchen as I stepped out of the shower dripping wet. I heard my ringtone go off suddenly. I knew that tone...I shot over to the night stand and grabbed my cell phone off it. Then I doubled back to the bedroom door, stuck my head out in search for Prina. She was in the kitchen. I pushed the door shut, pressed the send button and put the phone to my ear.

"Now just wait one god-damned minute, you don't call me, I call you, understand."

"Mr. Turner, you don't have to be so hostile so early in the morning. Have you had a hot cup?"

"You think this is funny. Well it's not. We've been over this, it's not safe. Why are you calling?"

"To congratulate you, Mr. Turner."

"For what?"

"Mr. Turner, you've done a wonderful job."

"Is that right?"...

"That's right man, hey why don't you come in so we can talk about it."

A Black Wall St. issued SUV suddenly pulled up into the driveway. Damn, it had to be Prince. I moved away from the window.

"Mr. Turner are you still there?"

"Yeah I'm here."

"Can you come in...say in the next 48 hours?"

"Don't call this number again."

"I heard you the first time, Mr. Turner."

"I just want us to be clear. When it's appropriate, I'll call you with a time. It'll be within the next 24 hours."

"Good Mr. Turner, we'll be waiting."

By the time I freshened up and got dressed, Prince was waiting inside the living room for me. He was nursing a hot cup of Prina's delicious coffee. Just this man's presence alone demanded respect. He carried himself as a person of importance. His presence was strong and often times very intimidating. I've always thought of myself in a similar manner, serious and shrewd when it came down to handling business. But for some reason, whenever I saw this cat, he had a way of making me feel uneasy. Every man should use direct eye contact when in a discussion, but Prince had this acute nature about him. I often got the impression that he could look straight through me.

He'd come by to insist that we all attend the service together. True indeed, I agreed that it was important that we be there. Regardless of the circumstances, I doubt if Pastor Rodney would approve of the disunity amongst the community. His whole life's work had been about enriching lives and bringing everyone together in the name of Jesus Christ. One senseless act of violence had compromised his great work. It seemed like the entire city of Richmond had come out to pay last minute respects to the beloved Pastor. Due to the expected crowd, which was in the thousands, the funeral service was held downtown at the James Center. I believe that the police department had prepared for violence to occur because they came out in full force. They were directing traffic and lingering around outside the building where at least two buses of swat team members were on standby. Many members of the Islam Nation had come out, believers with their wives and children. None of us stayed, we all simply walked through to view the body and lay flowers near our friend. The tension was more than obvious. Upon entering, it got so quiet that you could hear a pen hit the floor...But nothing happened, Thank God for that.

About the mysterious phone call early this morning. I was still livid about that damn thing. Instead of calling back within the 24 hour time frame as I'd intended, I decided to pull one of their numbers and pay them an unannounced visit. I took the necessary precautions as usual when meeting with these faceless wimps. No one had tailed me, I was sure of that. I wasted 20 minutes just burning gas around the city trying to delude any imaginary pursuers. Located on West Broad St, right around the corner from Willow Lawn Shopping Center, the building was tucked in between a Little Caesar's and Sally's Beauty supply store. To the unsuspecting public, it was a Nextel store that sold cell phones, but secretly it was a front for the FBI. It was approximately 4:20 in the evening time when I came to a complete stop 50 yards from the store after spotting two familiar faces that troubled me deeply. Tiffany Bullock and her brother Harry had just exited the very same establishment where I was headed...The Nextel store. What the hell was this? I had been on a relentless search for this girl ever since the Pastor's accident.

Brother Kihiem had put me on the mission. He said that she could possibly shed some light on his situation. When we first spoke, I thought the brother was delusional to think that there could somehow be a connection between his conversation with Tiffany and the Pastor's unfortunate accident. But now arriving and seeing her here had totally put a spin on things. I had spoke with her mom and everyone else who I thought she knew, but no one could confirm her whereabouts....until now. I watched them hurry from the building toward the parking lot. A scary thought is forming in my mind around this time. The Agent escorting Tiffany and Harry, I didn't recognize from any of my debriefings but strangely, I'd seen him before, but where? This guy moved with thorough efficiency and sharp alertness as he ushered Tiffany and Harry toward an unmarked dark tinted Quest Minivan.

I never forget a face. This Agent fella paused right outside the driver's door to do a last minute sweep of the parking lot.

It was then that I finally placed the guy's face. Instantly, the scary thought in my head had suddenly developed into horror. I knew exactly who this guy was. Though years had passed since, still I knew that face. It was like staring at a ghost. Never could I forget that strange white face on the track field that dreary morning in prison over several years ago. The morning I was stabbed nine times and left to die, I never believed for one minute that the Islam Nation had tried to off me in the can. But the administration or someone higher in authority, this was so unreal...It was just too much. Could it explain why on that early morning my assailants and I was the only people on the track? And it explains how they were able to hit me up and escape without a trace. Out of a population of seventeen hundred, no one saw these guys? Of course not, they escaped because the administration working in conjunction with the F.B.I (Counter Intel Agency) made it possible. I was the only one let out that morning. I jogged every morning around the same time. It wasn't a secret, everybody knew that. I didn't think anything of it when I looked around and saw no one... except for the strange white face, the decoy for my attacker who I never got a chance to see. But the white man, I swore that I'd take that image with me to my grave.

Many of us dismiss the idea of conspiracy theories for whatever reasons. But a lot of us are just not in tune with reality. There was no theory about what I'd just saw with my own two eyes. This was my life and it was going down. I needed answers now...Everything happening was somehow connected...I felt it.

Chapter

24

Percy "Prince" Miller

T
he four city officials, including one top ranking city councilman for the city of Richmond each repeating this notorious name over and over again as each of them carefully analyzed and dissected every bit of information documented in each personal file placed on the table before them. The present location was Washington, DC. FBI Headquarters. Quietly, each official thoroughly ingested the information provided to them by the city's top investigator with the Governors and Mayors upmost approval. In the very next room, was a special team of Agents solely dedicated to monitoring the affairs of the thriving giant, Black Wall St. On the bulletin board, were pictures of every Black Wall St. affiliate from the highest ranking official, down to the foot soldiers. In light of the current situation with the death of one of the key figures, a meeting was called. The file in front of each member was to be studied closely. Black Wall St. documents, the info contained every investor and their business ventures. Even the councilman as they viewed the material was impressed by the strategic moves and multimillion dollar investments of the business tycoon. McDonald Franchises, construction co, laundry mats; bulks of real estate and that was just scratching

the surface. The list went on and on. This Black Wall St. business was larger than life.

Instructions were given to stay the course. Pool every possible resource to shake up any potential Black Wall St. investors. **Operation Chaos**...Discourage them from investing in Black Wall St. projects and enhance media manipulation. Put the pedal to the medal and use every avenue to shake the very foundation of the Organization. Start with the head... Chop off the head, destroy the idea and everything else will fall in its proper perspective. With Preacher man dead and Brother Minister in jail and the community divided, **Operation Chaos** was right on schedule. But don't let up now; keep the momentum until the whole idea is totally obliterated. This was the focal point of the meeting.

There was Government and then there was the **"Shadow Government."** The real life Bad Boys who truly moved in silence, their faces were question marks and inside their smoke filled rooms, they blew cigar smoke and called shots...pulled strings like puppet masters. They were human predators. The poor and the ignorant were their prey, as well as any person who would so kindly attempt to enlighten the people. A divided people were easy to conquer and anyone seeking to change that was a threat. The **Bad Boys** sole purpose was to **Counter All Intelligence** rising up from within the black community. Catch it and kill it! Never allow the thought to become action.

"And this is why **Black Wall St.** has to cease to exist." The top investigator, Jack Daniels made that last statement very clear to everyone present before he was interrupted by his personal secretary.

She buzzed in. "Abby can it wait, I'm just finishing up here."

"Sir, I think you'll want to take this...it's from Virginia and it appears to be urgent."

Jack Daniels understood her tone. Indeed, it must be serious for her to interrupt such a highly anticipated meeting. He quickly excused himself assuring everyone as he made his exit from the conference room that he'd return shortly. He entered into his spacious office and shut the door behind him. There was a call waiting on line two from the Agency in Richmond, Virginia. He sat, hit the button and grabbed the phone placing it to his ear. Jack Daniels listened intently for a couple minutes until his ears could no longer take it.

"What the hell do you mean their missing? I do not wanna hear this shit. Do you realize what could happen if the wrong people see them?"

"Sir, it's only been 24 hours," explained his Agent.

"You sonovabitch, I told you not to let them out of your sight, what part of Protective Custody don't you understand?"

"You're absolutely right sir."

Jack Daniels drew in a deep breath while rubbing his temples. Maybe it wasn't as bad as it seemed. Maybe the kids were simply tired of being cramped up in some bored to death safe house and decided to go out for air. But 24 hours though? So much was at stake. Their lives, not to mention this highly sensitive case! If Tiffany and Harry bullock fell into the wrong hands...He didn't even want to think about it.

"Tim, do you have any idea where they could be. I don't have to remind you-

"I understand the seriousness of it, Sir," Tim Dunstan cut in. "To answer your question, no we don't have their location as of this moment but I assure you that we are on it. But hey, I did however find something interesting on our surveillance camera."

"I'm listening."

Agent Tim Dunstan told his Superior that while reviewing the surveillance tape from yesterday, a warning signal went off in his head. Parked approximately fifty yards from their base, he encountered a suspicious vehicle facing in the direction of the store. In running the license plate; he discovered that it was in fact a company issued vehicle belonging to one of their CIs. Though he had spoken to the C.I. prior about coming in for a debriefing, the C.I. never followed up on the phone call to schedule an exact time. But strangely, he shows up unannounced. And yet the call never came, which drew suspicion from Agent Tim Dunstan. He checked the time on the surveillance camera and found that coincidentally, the car was there at the exact same time that Agent Mac Author and the two CIs were leaving the building.

"What are you telling me Agent... that this Nathanial Turner fella could have our C.I's?"

"I'm simply stating the facts Sir. He was here and it's a strong possibility that he may have encountered the CI's... Not only that Sir, what if he recognized Mac Author?"

"From fifty yards away, I doubt it. Besides it's been almost seven years and even then, he only got a glimpse of Agent Mac Author. This is unacceptable, Agent. Against my better judgment, I went along with you on this. I vouched for you and you're making me look like a goddamned fool."

"But Sir," Agent Tim Dunstan started...

"No, now you listen. If your men had followed orders the first time, this wouldn't be happening. Nat Turner would be dead and our CI'Ss would still be in custody. You said that he could be of great significance to us, that's the only reason why the bastard was let out in the first place. Those were your words Agent Tim Dunstan. This sonovabitch is no longer an asset to us. He's become a liability. Now you find him before he blows this case. If he does, it's over for us! Do you hear me, it's over...I don't give a damn how you do it, just do it! Clean up the mess you've made...."

TO BE CONTINUED
THE GHOST

Other published works by The Ghost:

Tribulation Of A Ghetto Kid...The Street Bible,
Tales From Da Hood, the Anthology by The Ghost with Nikki Turner
Cold Blooded...The New Year's Day Massacre

Coming soon.... The sequel to his first smash hit, *Tribulation Of A Ghetto Kid...The Saga Continues.*

CPSIA information can be obtained at www.ICGtesting.com
Printed in the USA
BVOW010854111111

275875BV00001B/6/P